Julie Hilden graduated from Harvard, and earned a law degree at Yale and an MA in creative writing from Cornell. After several years of practicing law, she has now turned to writing full time. Her first book, a memoir entitled *The Bad Daughter*, was published by Algonquin Books, and she has also written for *Slate* magazine. She lives in New York City.

3

A novel

Julie Hilden

BLACK SWAN

3
A BLACK SWAN BOOK : 0 552 77177 5

First publication in Great Britain
Originally published in the United States by Plume,
a member of Penguin Group (USA) Inc.

PRINTING HISTORY
Black Swan edition published 2004

1 3 5 7 9 10 8 6 4 2

Copyright © Julie Hilden 2003

The right of Julie Hilden to be identified as the author of this
work has been asserted in accordance with sections 77 and
78 of the Copyright Designs and Patents Act 1988.

Set in 11/14½pt Melior by
Kestrel Data, Exeter, Devon.

Black Swan Books are published by Transworld Publishers,
61–63 Uxbridge Road, London W5 5SA,
a division of The Random House Group Ltd,
in Australia by Random House Australia (Pty) Ltd,
20 Alfred Street, Milsons Point, Sydney, NSW 2061, Australia,
in New Zealand by Random House New Zealand Ltd,
18 Poland Road, Glenfield, Auckland 10, New Zealand
and in South Africa by Random House (Pty) Ltd,
Endulini, 5a Jubilee Road, Parktown 2193, South Africa.

Printed and bound in Great Britain by
Cox & Wyman Ltd, Reading, Berkshire.

Papers used by Transworld Publishers are natural, recyclable
products made from wood grown in sustainable forests.
The manufacturing processes conform to the environmental
regulations of the country of origin.

ACKNOWLEDGMENTS

My heartfelt thanks to my terrific agent, Harvey Klinger; my wonderful editor, Trena Keating; and the very talented people at Plume Books, including Laura Blumenthal, Norina Frabotta, Brant Janeway, and Lucy Kim.

Special thanks to Stephen Glass, for more reasons than I could possibly list.

I am extremely grateful for the kindess, generosity, and skill of those who helped with French publication and translation – Larry Berger, Anouk Markovitz, Pierrette Fleutiaux; and Marie-Catherine Vacher and everyone at Actes Sud.

A grateful thank-you to all those who read and commented on, or otherwise helped with, the novel, my author photos, or my Web site – B. A., T. B., Pamela Buchbinder, D. B., Maria Dizzia, Henry Dunow, Hampton Fancher, Jason Furman, Russ Galen, Eve Gerber, Michael Glass, Susanna Green, Brandt Goldstein, Mohsin Hamid, Lisa Hamilton, D. K., Geoff Kloske, Dahlia Lithwick, Joanne Mariner, Jessica O'Connell, F. P., Garth Patil, Josh Pashman,

C. P., Gretchen Rubin, Melanie Thernstrom, W. T., K. W., Amy Zalman, and Seth Zalman. Thank you also to my colleagues at FindLaw.com, Diahann Reyes and Kent Williams, who were unfailingly kind and understanding throughout.

Thanks, finally, to the friends who supported me through three long years of writing; to my father; and to my mother, in memory and always.

3

Part 1

It is the first Saturday in August when I walk up to the porch of the summerhouse and see them. I am supposed to be in the city this weekend but my interview is canceled, the actor called out of town. I see them through the fan propped in the window, through the transparent blur of its blades.

She is moving on top of him slowly, with such concentration that though she faces the window, though she could look right at me, she does not. I am only a few feet away from her. I have never seen her before.

I watch her glossy brown hair shift on her shoulders, I watch her empty eyes as she moves on him with calculation, with slack lips, with nipples so erect that the areolae wrinkle around them – as she moves with such pleasure, really, that who could hate her in this moment?

To love her, to want to be her, to want to touch her, yes. But not to hate her, not in this.

I watch her, and watch, too, a sliver of Ilan's

narrow chest beneath her, its pattern of hair that breaks across his sternum. I can see the necklace sliding on his chest as they move, the tiny silver hand slipping back and forth, its touch faster and jerkier than Ilan's own smooth caresses – than the touch of his hand moving on her downy back.

For perhaps five minutes, I don't say a word. It seems a weird privilege: here is the life I don't see, the life that goes on without me. I watch them as a ghost watches the living.

Then I say his name slowly, just audibly. She starts and looks around wildly. When she looks through the fan and sees me, she gasps.

Ilan does not start at all; not a flicker. But he lifts his head, sees me, and winces, and just like that he lifts her off him and at the same time off the bed.

'You have to go now,' he tells her.

She dresses insolently slowly. Her blouse fastens in the back with a line of ties – it is really just a square of cloth that settles on her breasts – and she loops each of the ties into a perfect bow.

'Fuck you,' she tells Ilan. 'You fucking liar. I deserve better than you.' Righteous anger, but controlled.

She and I brush past each other in the doorway. She is the woman I am supposed to be: a hair tosser, a thrower of water from glasses, a slapper, a terrific girl all told. Dignified, she slips through the high reeds near the driveway and begins to walk along

12

the road slowly, carrying her pretty embroidered shoes. She does not look back at him, at us, at the house for even a moment, because she knows what she deserves.

It's as if she's preempted me with her anger; I want to shout at Ilan too, curse at him, but I don't have the heart. 'I should leave too,' is all I say.

'You can't leave me, Maya. I love you.'

'Was this the first time – the only time? I need to know.'

'It started in college,' he admits, 'a few weeks after I met you.'

I shiver. I never expected to be chosen by myself, for myself alone. It had felt wrong – unlike me – to be chosen. Now, hearing this, I feel only a sickening familiarity, not surprise.

'It never meant anything,' he assures me. 'I felt awful about it. I don't know where it comes from. I thought, with enough therapy, I'd talk myself out of it. But all I do is confess, I don't change. Look, can we at least sit down? I feel like any moment, you're going to leave.'

'Okay, but I'm not promising to stay.'

I sit down on the rattan couch. He stands behind me. I lean back and reach my head up to him – like a rabbit in a cage straining to sip from its water dispenser, the single round, hanging drop. And he leans down, princelike, to kiss me.

Then he starts to touch me. He slips his hands

down my jeans, his fingers splayed, rubbing my clitoris insistently, with the slightest pressure. I moan quietly, move against him.

'Don't I know you?' he says. 'I know exactly what you want, don't I?'

It agitates me as he rubs and rubs, softly, softly. He touches me the way he learned from me years ago – the way I touch myself. He studied it. The detail of his knowledge of me devastates. If I were to close my eyes, I could confuse his touch with my own.

But as he nuzzles into my shoulder, I smell sex in his hair and break away from him.

'Would you at least shower?' I demand.

'No, you love that. Tell me you love it.'

In seconds my jeans are gone, my shirt is gone. He holds on to me, won't let me leave.

'It's so soft,' he says as he touches me. 'You're so wet.'

He gets a little bleat out of me as he rubs. Then I clamp my mouth shut. Ah, but then I relax it. I begin to breathe in the sex smell in his hair; I begin almost to like it.

'Maya. Tell me you want this.'

'I want it.'

'I knew you did.' And I do. And it is hours, then, before we can stop.

*   *   *

Early that evening, I return to the city alone. As I walk away from our house to meet the bus, I look back and see the fan there in the window, its blades spinning in the same blur. I imagine that again I can look through it and see the girl, moving up and down so slowly, her breasts bare.

At our loft, I am alone for days – for so long that I feel as if I should be taking a plane somewhere; only plane trips have separated us for this many days before. Ilan calls and leaves messages every day, but I don't pick up. I only listen to his voice, trying to assess what he says as if I were a stranger, someone objective. I notice that he never promises to be faithful; he only begs to see me. He says he loves me, and he wants me back.

As I lie on the bed we share, I feel as if my chest bones should be opened like a doored cage, and my heart displayed so that someone can say 'Enough.' I cry my mascara off, cry it into black rivulets on my face and leave it that way.

Then I try an experiment. I kneel on our bed and brace myself against the wall as if I were above Ilan. I close my eyes to visualize his face, imagining the silver hand on its chain shifting on his chest as he strains beneath me. I test, in the most visceral way I can, whether I can withstand his being gone.

Part 2

I am nineteen when it begins – a sophomore. Outside the college library, I lean against one of its huge columns, my bookbag at my feet, waiting for my roommate. Ilan, then a stranger, walks up to me and asks, 'Are you waiting for me?'

'I might be,' I tell him. I am not much for this kind of flirtation, but today, he brings it out of me.

Ilan is tall, rangy, narrow-hipped and leather-jacketed, with brown-black hair and dark circles under his eyes. Around his neck he wears a small silver hand on a chain, with a ruby set into its finger.

I lift the chain from his neck; the tiny hand rests in my palm. The world falls away for a moment. I imagine the figure the hand would belong to: a ruby-eyed god that would curl in the notch of Ilan's collarbone, a tiny familiar.

'My grandmother gave it to me,' Ilan says, and touches my arm – the first of a light rain of touches. 'It's the hand of God. It's supposed to protect me.'

'Has it?'

'Yeah,' he says. 'It has.' He smiles.

'Then I wish I had one too. I need the protection,' I say, surprising myself; I don't usually admit need, and I don't even know him. But too quickly for me to protest, he lifts the chain from his neck and puts it around mine.

The next morning I arrive at his room to return the chain. He answers the door unshaven, a towel around his waist, his hair wet. I take a nervous step backward, and hold the chain out to him.

'I kept thinking I was going to lose it,' I explain.

'I knew it would be fine, but it's nice to have it back.' He reaches to take it from me and fastens it around his neck again. 'It was the first time I'd taken it off.'

Ilan asks me to meet him for a drink that evening, and after that we stay up all night, many nights, talking. During this time I, who love sleep, rarely sleep. Ilan calls the resulting state 'exhaustion ecstasy' – the relaxation that arises from deep tiredness, the exquisite weariness of every limb and the sailing feeling that accompanies it.

We'll outlast everyone else in Ilan's dormitory room or mine, watching them go to sleep one by one, until they leave us alone with each other. 'I can't wait until we can be alone,' he'll whisper.

Or some nights we'll go to the one café in town

that never closes and choose a plush sofa to share, take our shoes off and settle in. I slip my toes into the space between Ilan's thigh and the couch cushion as we talk.

Soon I trust him enough to sleep with him. He is my third lover. Unlike the previous two, he reaches me. His voice on the phone revs up my heart instantly, setting it beating fast. In bed he is a revelation, yet also something already known.

His hair is short and soft, when it seems it should be stubble, should be prickly. I want to touch it all the time. When he is inside me, I put my legs around him, arch my feet, and match the curve of each arch to the curve of the back of one of his calves, fitting us together.

He goes down on me and says it is like kissing me. He picks a lock of pain and pleasure, of shame and want – waiting patiently as if he were listening for each of a safe's tumblers to fall into place. When he touches my breasts, he alternates between cupping the entire breast firmly and pinching, with two fingers, each nipple, and I begin to believe I have always wanted to be touched this way. Whether he changes me or reveals me, I have difficulty telling.

My pleasure is acute and it hurts me to have it. It comes to me on narrow beds in dormitory rooms, or on the desks of closed classrooms we slip into, through windows or unlatched doors, late at night.

It comes to me with bark scratching at my back, through my sweater – as I stand for Ilan in the dark in a forest near campus, my skirt up, and he, on his knees, opens me. It comes to me loudly and softly, and all the time. It is something he can give to me, take from me, anywhere. He is the one key that always opens.

One night he makes me show him how I touch myself. My habit is to rub myself on my palm, facedown. For the longest time, embarrassed, I refuse to let him watch. But eventually I do show him.

After that, he often asks me to lie facedown so that he can lie on top of me and put his hand under mine as I touch myself, copying the motion. This makes me come in a moment, until I cry with it. It is so exciting simply that he wants to know how to do this, and that I let him learn.

Ilan loves to startle me out of my stillness, to make me cry out. I begin to depend on him for it. How close can you get? We try to run the body out to the end of its endurance, having sex over and over, as if there is some boundary we are closing in on, but can never touch.

I give myself over to him and wait for that delicious feeling of falling. But even as I relax, I know there is still a brake in me – like the twitch and jerk of threat that ends that falling feeling in light sleep, rousing me awake. I can feel his palms on me, my back can arch; still I keep that tiny mooring, like the handle on the end of a kite string. That little catch in me: if I lost it, I would lose myself entirely.

Before I meet Ilan, I live in my mind. I have been this way since childhood: the stillest girl, the one who waits quietly. As a child, I notice that adults forget I am in the room; they talk over my head. Older now, I remain quiet, full of my unrealized wants. Most of the time I do not even begin a thing, because, even starting out, I can see so acutely its impossibility.

This is what I desire most in life: a dream platform. There, two people would exist in the same space – as if on an empty white stage – and be able to speak and act with complete candor, enact their true desires.

Afterward, both people would remember the dream but would not be able to allude to it. They would simply know about it emotionally, with the kind of knowledge you can never put into words.

Life falls short whenever I compare it to the life I imagine might happen on the dream platform – and so, until I meet Ilan, I barely live at all. I don't speak in class, and rarely speak elsewhere. My two room-mates have lived with me since the first day of freshman year, but they know little about me. They might notice things – I'll row by myself; I don't have much money; if men chase me, I always cut things off after a few dates – but I know these traits don't quite jell into a personality.

Even my parents hardly know me now. Long ago I stepped neatly out of my family – that is, my families. After their divorce when I was three, my parents both remarried and had other children: five apiece, two broods much younger than I. They are happy kids, brought up that way, as I was brought up in fighting. Now my parents have adopted a sort of willed amnesia about that unhappy, angry time. Good for them, in my opinion: who would want to dwell there? I was all too happy, myself, to escape it – through books, or solitary walks, or simply by imagining myself elsewhere, in some better life.

I'm my parents' guest whichever home I go to, like a spinster aunt. I am the mistaken child, the changeling. Half sister to all, sister to none. On the margin of other people's lives, I am a character who enters and exits, whose disappearance can be afforded, can be borne. I am far from the favorite of either of my parents, nor am I that of any teacher, grandparent, or friend. No one marks me out to say: you.

And as much as anyone learns about me, I always think there is some deeper privacy in me they can never reach. I delight in thinking shocking things yet betraying nothing, to prove to myself again and again that I will not be known.

Yet somehow Ilan knows me. And he chooses me, chooses me alone, above all others.

A few weeks after we begin dating, Ilan drives me out to my mother and stepfather's house in Connecticut for Thanksgiving dinner. He wears a jacket and tie. I play my CDs loudly and want the car trip never to end. We make each other laugh so hard he swerves.

Over drinks, my meticulous, beautiful mother snipes at me: 'Maya, that sweater has a pull in it. Why aren't you taking care of your clothes?'; 'You know, having a boyfriend doesn't mean you're excused from studying.'

We aren't there for an hour before Ilan makes an excuse – we are going to the grocery store – and rescues me.

'The store's that way,' I instruct him once we're in the car.

'We're not going there,' he tells me. 'Is there someplace we can be alone?'

'There's a field in back of the elementary school.'

When I was growing up, I used to lie by myself in that field often in the fall, beneath the leaves that lay thick on the grass as they do now – a submerged child who watched the sky. I imagined myself underwater, as if the leaves floated on a pond's surface, and I floated just beneath.

Once we arrive, I try to kiss Ilan, but he shakes his head. 'Come over here,' he says.

We scuff leaves, walking, and he leads me to a thick, low-hanging tree branch. The northern edge of the field is lined with twisted trees that crane and reach. Of them all, this is the easiest to climb.

'It's the best tree,' I tell him, and he nods.

I clamber up to sit on the branch and then I drop myself upside down, releasing first one hand and then the other, until I am hanging by my knees, the way I used to as a child here.

'Your mother is something else,' he says.

'Wait until you meet my father.' I hitch myself back up to a sitting position.

'He's just as bad?'

'Only to me. You have to understand, they hate each other, and I was the child of their marriage. And they're both perfectionists – it was why they divorced. They like the pretty families they have now. I think they wish I didn't exist.'

'It's not normal, Maya.'

'Normal or not, that's the way it is. Is your family so normal? You never talk about them.'

'There's not much to say, it's only my father now. My mother died when I was eight. It was pancreatic

26

cancer – no warning, and she was gone in two months.'

Ilan climbs up to join me on the branch. He rearranges me so I am leaning against his chest. Settling back against him, I look out onto the eddies of yellow and orange leaves.

'The month before she died was like a siege in our house – nurses, sometimes a doctor too. My father was set on her never going to the hospital, and he was sick too. Nothing the doctor could diagnose, I think he just wanted to die when she did. So it was like I had no parents. The nurses kept telling me what to do, and I kept ignoring them.

'There was an IV for my mother, with painkillers. By the end, she was taking enormous doses. She'd tell me about her hallucinations. Dreams of falling or flying. I used to believe they were my dreams too. Once I was talking about one of them, this particularly great dream of flying over New York so you could see Central Park and all, and my father corrected me. He said it sternly, like, "That's your *mother's* dream." Like, "Give that back to your mother."

'Before she got sick, we had this game. We'd tell each other a real dream and a made-up one. The other person had to guess which was which.'

He twists a lock of my hair around one of his fingers as he talks, tensing the curl.

'After she got sick, I'd always sleep in her bed. If the nurse kicked me out, I'd sleep underneath, right on the marble. Anyway, one night I was reading to her, and I fell asleep. I woke up the next morning and her face was gray. No one expected it. She'd been feeling better – maybe a remission, the doctor said. No one thought it would be that night. The doctor apologized, he was embarrassed. We'd missed her death.'

He pauses. I understand that he does not want me to twist around to see his face. It is possible that as he talks, he is soundlessly crying, but if that is the case I will never know it. Throughout my time with Ilan, I never see him cry.

'I've told that story so many times to shrinks, I don't even feel it anymore,' he says quietly. 'It was such a powerful feeling, and now I've lost it. There was a talk we were going to have before she died, she said so. But the last thing she said to me was, "You need to wash your hair."'

We are silent for a moment. Then I ask him, 'How was it with your father afterward?'

'Okay. At least he made an effort. He got himself out of bed the day she died and made me an omelet. It wasn't cooked all the way through but I ate it anyway. He missed my mother but we didn't talk about it much. But I used to talk to her in my head. Sometimes I still do. I feel like I learn more about her every year.

'Well, that's my mother, that's the story,' he says abruptly. 'Let's go. Your parents are going to think we were in an accident.'

'I don't care what they think.'

He helps me down from the branch, carrying me in his arms for a moment. I cannot tell if he has been crying, but as usual his eyes are big and dark; they take in the world.

Ilan drives us back to the house. After an hour with him outside as a respite, for once I am not lonely there. I can act like a guest – drying my hands with my mother's monogrammed towels, keeping my napkin in my lap and my elbows off the table, making sure to use the correct silverware. My life is elsewhere.

The next day, my mother calls me at school to say she believes Ilan's a good influence, protective. But she doesn't know that what he protects me from is her – her happiness with her other children, and her odd formality with me.

The party's very dark and our cigarette ends, like fireflies, leave trails in the air. The off-campus apartment is lit only by candlelight and moonlight, with a balcony that people drift onto, and then drift back from. The darkened French doors that lead there reflect the many different candle flames inside, and their translucent curtains balloon when the wind catches them.

Everyone is drunk, dancing with abandon. I stand close to Ilan in a corner, and accidentally I touch my cigarette to his arm.

'Sorry,' I whisper.

'Try it again.' But I won't, I hesitate.

'You won't hurt me,' he assures me.

I touch him again. He doesn't flinch.

'Try it for longer.' I hold the cigarette close to his skin and watch as it begins to blister.

'Okay, stop' – he says it a beat later than I expect. And I wait that beat, I wait for him to speak.

Then he does it to me, burns me a little. After an instant, I whimper at him, indignant, 'Stop.' Tears come to my eyes.

We begin to alternate. It is a game. 'Ouch,' I hiss, when it is my turn. And in a second, he stops. But when it is his turn, he can take the pain silently, and even smile at me as I burn him, as if to say, 'What is this to me?'

He waits longer each time, so calm. I wonder what quality in him makes him able to wait. It seems a spiritual quality, like the ability to walk on coals – one I envy.

Soon a small circle of people forms around us, two men – one large and one small – and a woman. We mesmerize them. Glassy-eyed in the dark room, they watch me put the cigarette on Ilan's skin, watch it blister. Showing off, he no longer tells me when to stop; he lets me decide when.

'Do that again,' the large man commands, but Ilan refuses.

Frustrated with Ilan, the men begin burning each other. Drunk, they drop cigarettes and laugh, fall against things and swear.

Their adoption of our game seems menacing: it was between us, about us. Ilan and I draw together and slip out onto the balcony, into the moonlight and the full, cool blast of night air.

Through the glass-paned door we can see the small man drop an ember on the woman's skirt, the fabric scorching around the hole it leaves. It is hard to tell if he has done it intentionally, to bring her into the game. She screeches, and the large man, tall in a light blue jacket like a jazz musician's, threatens the small man, who tells him to fuck off.

In an instant, the large man pushes the small one against the balcony door. Glass shatters all at once, falling in a quick, brutal hail. The party's host shouts, 'They're going to make me pay for that.'

The small man steps back from the door with one of his hands bloody – his thumb has a shard of glass in it. The woman pries out the splinter and rips off part of the hem of her ruined skirt to bind the thumb. But the moment the bleeding stops, the small man is at it again, smearing his bloody hand on the large man's blue jacket, and she backs away from both of them in disgust.

31

'Let's go,' Ilan whispers to me. He puts his arm around my shoulder and guides me safely out.

Back in Ilan's dormitory room, we curl together to sleep – but for once I cannot drift off in his arms. I intensely need a cigarette but I've run out.

I don't wake him, don't want to admit my need. He always takes my last cigarette, believing I am not addicted the way he is. And that's what I let him believe – that I can wait.

It's not true, not now at least. Though it's the middle of the night, I go out by myself to the convenience store, nonchalantly shoving the pack into my pocket after I pay, so even the clerk won't know the extent of my desire.

Outside Ilan's door I smoke quickly, almost desperately. Then I go back in, brush my teeth with his toothbrush, and slip back into bed.

The next day, we hear the fight got out of control. One guy's arm was broken; the woman was badly burned. And the day after that, we receive phone calls from the college, telling us there will be a disciplinary hearing. Official letters soon arrive. It turns out the woman is claiming the fight was our fault.

Ilan's father gets a lawyer to represent us both. He is portly and officious, unhappy to be here. Ilan and I are told we have the right to separate, private hearings, but instead we ask to attend each other's – which are scheduled on the same day. I don't tell my parents what is happening.

On the appointed day, we sit in a huge, echoey lecture hall in uncomfortable wooden chairs whose arms hold podlike half desks. Facing us, on an elevated podium, is a panel of three old, sober faces and two eager young ones, those of fellow students.

Ilan stands; he is to speak first. 'I hope we aren't going to get burned,' he remarks, and smiles.

No one smiles back. Even I don't dare. The lawyer glares at him, and he flinches.

'Sit down, Mr Resnick, until you can take this seriously,' the head of the panel, an elderly woman, intones. 'Ms Sumner, why don't we move on to you.'

I rise to stand before the panel.

'Why do *you* think you did it, Maya?' the woman asks.

I sense that she wants to let me off, since I'm only a girl, after all. And I know what I should say, what the lawyer has coached us to say: we are very sorry for any harm we caused, and we learned from the experience never to do this again. But I find I can't say it. What Ilan and I learned was different – more interesting, more dangerous – and I don't believe we caused any harm. I don't want to lie.

'I don't think it's any of your business,' I tell her, surprised at how hostile I sound. 'We didn't hurt

33

anyone. Why don't you blame the guy who started the fight?'

'He'll have a hearing too. This is yours. Is there anything you want to say? Any explanation you'd like us to consider, maybe an apology you'd like to offer?'

'No.' I shrug and, without permission, I sit down.

The lawyer gives me a frustrated, furious look and leans over to whisper instructions to Ilan. But Ilan, when he is called upon, follows my lead and refuses to speak.

We are two stubborn children, nineteen and twenty. In the end, we are expelled. It is hard to blame the school, for we have been so uncooperative. Even so, the letters we receive say we can reapply in a year or two – as long as we get the counseling we need to prepare ourselves for the 'adult situation' of college.

We know we won't return. Scoffing at the letters, Ilan burns them, setting them alight in a small metal dish. It takes a long time, but we watch them disappear into ash.

It occurs to me, when I learn we will be leaving, that there have been some real violations of which, ironically, the college never learned.

Though I try not to admit it to myself, I have started to write Ilan's papers for him sometimes. The writing comes easily to me, and only with difficulty to him, so gradually I move from commenting on his papers, to editing them, to simply writing them myself for him to submit.

The evolution is quick, and we never talk about it; it simply happens. One night he leaves to have dinner with friends, and when he returns I have finished his work for him. He only smiles and says, 'Good, now we have the rest of the night to ourselves.'

We still discuss the papers as if it were he, and not I, who had written them. I even overhear him boast, to his father, of the good grades he's begun to receive. I don't mind: I am happy that there is one way in which I can save him, since I feel he has saved me in so many ways.

And I already accept that we will never be like other people – will never live like other people. It is not that I believe the rules don't apply to us, it is that I believe we will have another way of living, one that lies somewhere outside normal life. And so I wonder whether leaving college, for others our age a catastrophe, may in the end be for us a strange triumph, a mark of how far we have departed.

I spend the time I would have spent preparing for spring exams with Ilan's hands in my hair, cupping my skull, as I move above him; as he teaches me my own pleasure by degrees. You were my education, Ilan – the one I preferred.

I walk through libraries of cramming students, heads bent over their desks, mumbling formulas they have memorized. As my roommates study, I pack my belongings in cardboard boxes, unsure where I'll send them. I am more excited than afraid.

Our plans for the future are settled quickly, almost instantly. Ilan's father offers us summer internships at the magazine where he works, in the city, and we move into a beautiful triangular loft he owns in Tribeca.

On the second story of a warehouse building, the loft is accessible only by a small, private factory elevator. It has five sets of huge floor-to-ceiling windows that face the street, so in the daytime it is filled with sunlight. The windows are made of thick double-paned glass, so that they block out virtually all outside noise. Heavy locks – including one that can be opened and closed only from the inside – will keep us safe there.

Ilan and I sleep in the broad bedroom at the triangle's base. A smaller bedroom at its apex becomes a writing room we share. Eventually, it seems to me, that room will be perfect for a child.

I am amazed and intimidated by the life Ilan and his father have given me. I know that on my own I would be temping, not writing – and I would barely be able to make enough money to live anywhere in the city, let alone here.

I am relieved to be able to tell my parents about my new job and apartment at the same time I break the news to them, belatedly, of my expulsion. My mother mutters, but she does not yell – and she stops hounding me to return to school, after a while. She knows Ilan's family is prominent, and that is probably why she drops the subject.

Ilan's father's magazine is small but growing, a sort of younger brother to *GQ* and *Vanity Fair*. Ilan mentioned earlier that his father worked there, but now I learn he owns the magazine as well.

I start my job the week after Mr Resnick offers it to me. My only qualification is that Ilan chose me; now his father chooses me too.

The magazine's building is located in west Chelsea, only a few subway stops away from our apartment. Ilan and I share a tiny office there, our desks facing. It is as if we are one person, almost never seen apart. I am one of only a handful of female staff writers, and the men stay far away from me, probably because I date the boss's son.

The job is surprisingly easy – Ilan's father feeds us stories, and I find that simply saying the magazine's name over the phone makes people who would never speak to me reveal their secrets. I am entranced. I understand then, at nineteen, that I will never do anything else but write, for as long as people let me.

My expulsion begins to seem like a mere shortcut,

a clever side road into the life I would have longed for anyway.

After work, Ilan and I spend most of our time alone together in the loft. We have sex almost every night there, and eventually we begin to experiment.

Often Ilan ties me up and I twist below him with my wrists together, pinioned on the cold bed frame. He has carefully untangled the braid of the belt that encircled the waist of his silk robe, and now he likes to use its three strands of silk to tie me up. They are soft but they pull tight; often I have no room to slip my hands out, and I am helpless.

Once, I tie him up instead. He gives me two arms with which to start, letting me tie them to the bed frame. Then I tie his legs apart too.

'Untie me,' he commands.

'Why?'

'It doesn't turn me on when it's me.'

'I'll go down on you,' I offer.

'I still won't like it. Untie me.'

I want to watch him in that position longer, the position where everything powerful about him falls away. But I begin to untie him instead.

As the first arm is freed, Ilan relaxes. When the second is freed, he sits up and begins to untie his legs himself, pushing me away when I try to help him. When he is done, he springs up from the bed and throws the cords onto the floor.

Afterward it is me he ties up. If he is particularly rough with me that night, I understand why. He knots the ties hard, without any room to slip my wrists out. I will not have his privilege, that of changing my mind.

Ilan tells me he wants to do everything with me: everything in life, everything sexually. Even as it makes me happy to hear it, I wonder what that will mean, and soon I find out.

One night, he asks me to have sex with him 'a different way.' Even knowing what he must mean, I reluctantly say I will.

I lie on my side and Ilan lies on his side next to me. I am very afraid of the pain I anticipate, but I concentrate on relaxing my breathing, my body, as he tells me I must.

He enters me just slightly and I close around him. I watch the huge, curtained window of our bedroom. I wince as he softly kisses the back of my neck. I can hear children's voices, from the playground across the street. I think, They cannot possibly even intimate what will happen to them when they grow up. I think, They are blind.

'You need to relax,' Ilan says again. I feel a new anxiety though, for I know this has to happen; he wants it for the sense of possession, because I did not lose my virginity with him, and also for the shame: I am to turn that over to him.

'Relax, I won't hurt you,' he says. 'I have all the time in the world.'

As he pushes inside me, I can feel the small negotiation of muscle, feel him calibrating when he will hurt me and stopping precisely at that point. It is so erotic, it almost makes me cry.

It is this moment, perversely, that finally convinces me to trust him completely. Over all the years we do this, I never bleed. The point is that he knows he can make me; and he refrains.

One day later that summer, Ilan and I take the subway up to the Museum of Natural History to see an exhibit, a roomful of butterflies. The butterfly-arium, Ilan calls it; there is some formal name, too, that I now forget.

Once admitted, we walk gingerly, in case the butterflies alight on the floor. We wait patiently for them to settle on our clothes or hair or hands. It feels like waiting for a kind of grace, against high odds. But for each of us, one alights.

We hold out our sleeves to compare them. Mine is a dark blue swallowtail whose wings bear spots like eyes and narrow into long, pendulous ends as they slowly open and close. His is an orange-and-black monarch, glamorous and quotidian, its markings brilliant as a peacock's and characteristic as a tabby's.

Our life is like that then. It simply comes to us

like grace, like a gift. I remember it all, you know. I would rather not remember it but I do. I remember how still I held for the butterfly; I remember exactly the way it dipped in the air when it flew away.

I remember it because Ilan was there, because that was how magical life seemed when I was with him. I still wonder, How can it have all gone so wrong?

Although I know it all did happen, because I lived it, I still do not fully believe that it is really over. In my mind, always, I am still beginning it. The butterfly is still alighting. There is still a world that comes to me so easily, so weightlessly, without a trail of blood.

At the end of the summer, Ilan and I are offered permanent jobs at the magazine, and we accept them. His father sees no problem with our deciding not to return to school. He did not attend college himself, he points out, yet he hires Ivy League graduates every year. The world itself will educate us, he tell us.

And Ilan, I believe, will educate me too; I borrow his books and read them methodically. I even read books from his childhood that he has by now forgotten, trying to intuit how they shaped him, made him the person I love and not some other person.

My mother voices her unhappiness, but I don't listen. As a result, she begins to concentrate even more on her other daughters: one a freshman at Yale, one applying to college, one soon to apply. All three are like Goldilocks; all of life, for each, is Just Right.

At the magazine, I begin to profile celebrities. I have a neat, meticulous approach to my job. My mother, if she knew how I worked, would be proud.

First I collect all the past coverage, all the major articles. In each, I underline in Hi-Liter any quote or fact that seems off base. Then I read the highlighted material over and over, until I have an image of the celebrity different from what the public sees, a sort of shadow image made up of all the small, disconcerting details and comments that have slipped through.

I try to hold that image in my mind, and during the interview, it is that person to whom I believe I speak.

I want the interviews to be like small traps into which the subject steps unknowing, so I concentrate on minutiae about which the celebrity has never been closely questioned. I ask about acquaintances, not friends; about an uncharacteristic dress, or an object that does not fit with the others in the celebrity's house. Or I ask three different variants of a single, crucial question, peppering them through the interview. In this way, I sometimes get the truth.

I use this method because I believe people betray

themselves. My method leads to strange interviews. At best they are unusual, revealing. I press upon lives to try to find out where their stress fractures are. Perhaps, unconsciously, I already intuit the invisible fractures in my own.

The next summer, we rent a house upstate. It is small and white, with a lawn of reeds that ripple like water when the wind blows.

There, we separate during the day and write, then reconvene in the evening for dinner. Everything seems easy and slow. I stop smoking, doing so easily and without struggle. I surprise myself because I find I can wish away my need after all – the same need that persists in Ilan whenever he tries to quit.

During the warm nights, the overhead spinning fan clicks as its blades turn – it rocks in its socket as it cools us – and a second fan, which we place in the front window, blows over our bodies as we sleep.

We keep the ancient black-and-white TV the owners leave, so every movie we rent is black-and-white for us. We freeze Coca-Cola into Popsicles and pry them from their cold-sticky metal trays. Exploring the attic, we flush out birds and even bats, watching them screech and wing away.

We live in the past; we live alone. We live in the perfect quiet of our thoughts, our work, and the love that for each of us is ultimate, definitive. We are in our early twenties; yet perhaps we are already there.

*　　*　　*

On the 4th of July, we drive to Ilan's father's summer place in East Hampton. Ilan has traveled into the city the previous day to buy fireworks illegally in Chinatown. Now, on the expanse of his father's dark lawn, they twist and hiss and sputter before us in throes of light.

Two of Ilan's cousins are there for the holiday, twin girls who are eight years old. I can tell Ilan prefers the quieter of the two – the one who reads a book and hangs back – and has no time for her aggressive twin. The one he chooses is the little girl I was.

She burns herself with her sparkler. It confirms for her, I think, that she should stay inside with her books. She runs crying into the house. Her sister stays on the lawn outside, waving her sparkler overhead – crowned by its short lines of white, perpendicular light.

Inside the house, the girl Ilan prefers has a fresh red burn on her hand. He opens her small hand to run it under water.

'It's going to be all better,' he tells her. 'Count aloud with me, and each number is going to make it better.'

She starts counting, and by the time she is at seven, she has stopped crying and he's drying off her hand.

Then Ilan sits with her on the staircase and talks

to her about her book. Their conversation is quick magic; he challenges her, takes her seriously.

'Why is she your favorite character?' I listen to him ask the girl intently, and I hear her quietly explain.

It is that day that I understand that as young as I was when we met, as young as I still am, this is not a passing romance: it is the love I will have, the love I'll choose. I believe, as I watch them, that the little girl will remember the conversation always – literally remember only the sparkle and the burn, but also intimate a conversation she cannot quite recall. Her cousin said something important; it is not recoverable; she tries to remember it but she cannot.

Ilan, I almost believe you came to me that way in childhood – sat with me after fireworks until I fell asleep, and then disappeared. I almost believe you chose me and changed me long ago, spoke to me and convinced me of something that went deep but that I immediately forgot. But then I remember it is only a dream of mine. You did not come to me then, and your appearance in my life later was not a magical thing, even if it has felt that way to me at times.

Shall I say those months, those years, that we were happy? I am not sure what that means. At the time I believed we were, but looking back I am no longer so certain.

It is a month later, in mid-August, when I find

45

Ilan with the other woman, when I watch them through the window. It is then that I discover my life is very different from the life I imagined it to be, and our happiness is not as pure as it appears.

'I'm not going to leave,' I tell Ilan, on the night I allow him to return to the loft. It is the middle of August, a week after I found him with the woman, after I watched them through the window. It has been a week of his messages, and of my silence.

'I won't even ask you to be faithful,' I announce. 'You can be with other women.'

'You're sure?' he asks, but he is not really asking. He pushes down the pockets of his hooded sweatshirt and looks at me, assessing me to see if I am serious. He sits down next to me on the couch.

'Yes, I'm sure.'

He nods. I think it long ago clicked with him that this was the only way for us to live. He had been waiting, hoping I would reach the same conclusion.

'You have to promise you'll always tell me the truth,' I warn him. 'There can't be anything I don't know about.'

'Of course.'

'And I have to always be there.'

He blanches, looks at me astonished. 'What?'

'It's the only way. Otherwise I'll always think you're falling in love with someone else.'

I've thought about this a long time, and I have

tried to be as severe with myself as I can, to find out if I really will be able to bear it. It is as I told him: I can't see another way. I know it is not in him to be faithful. I believe I can live with this bargain. And privately, I have to confess to myself that there is even a little allure mixed in with the pain I know I can expect. A darker life, I have begun to hope, can have its pleasures too.

'Fine, I agree,' he says. He thinks for a moment, and then he looks at me almost quizzically, hopeful the way a child is hopeful, and he goes down on one knee, next to the couch, and produces a ring.

He is tall enough that even kneeling, he is still large to me, but more vulnerable. I can see close up the sharp, white part that divides his soft, dark hair.

'Will you marry me?' he asks.

'No. Not this way.'

'Maya, you just explained, this is the only way it can be. And you're right. Don't you love me?'

'Of course I do.'

'Then marry me. The only obstacle is gone. You took it away. Please, marry me.'

'All right,' I say quietly. It is a flaw in me; I love that surrendering moment.

The diamond is so big it is embarrassing, and I make Ilan exchange it for a smaller one. He tells me with glee, though, that the new, smaller diamond is more precious: a yellow diamond, particularly rare and costly. It seems strangely ugly to me – tainted or aged. But I am too tired to argue, to tell him to take it back again. This time, I just tell him it's beautiful.

And so it is that we are to be married in splendor. The wedding, we decide, will take place the following spring. Ilan promises I can count on his fidelity until then; the bargain between us won't take effect until we actually marry. Meanwhile, he devotes himself to planning.

'You don't have to do this,' I tell Ilan as he orders tablefuls of orchids, as he selects the violinists who will rove the reception. 'I feel like you're trying to make it up to me. Aren't my parents supposed to pay?'

'I love you, and I can easily afford this. I want you to have a beautiful wedding.'

His eyes shine. It strikes me: he had not thought he could ever marry.

I have faith in him – there, I've said it. I believe in him. Even if it makes me a fool to do so, I am willing to be a fool.

How is it that faith can be explained, the feeling of it? You fall asleep in a room with a window on the sea. When you wake – having slept deeply, undisturbed – you cannot know, but you still feel, that the sea continued all night. You can almost hear all the hours when it lapped at the shore as you slept; that is how strongly you believe in the sea, how deeply the waves' sound convinced you. You believe the sea waited for you as you slept, like a lover who stays up breathing beside you, watching you through the night.

Although I know it may be impossible, given the bargain I've made, it is only a few days after we get engaged that I start to daydream of having a child. All my life I've dreamed of impossible things – another family, another self – and this, it turns out, is no different.

Growing up, I never thought I would want a child. But when I was eighteen I changed my mind. It happened when one of my half sisters gave birth secretly, during her sophomore year of high school – one of the perfect daughters not so perfect after all.

I was a freshman in college, home for a vacation during the year before I met Ilan, when I still hung around my family like an uneasy ghost. I was brought along to the birth because my mother wanted me to drive – she and my sister would ride in the backseat, she told me, and I would drive them home when it was all over.

I remember that my mother held my sister's hand as she went into labor, and in her other hand, my sister held a push button by which she could control the amount of painkiller, within limits the doctor had set. The button seemed to comfort her; she adjusted it by tiny amounts as if to convince herself the drug was still there if she needed it.

After many hours of labor, she was told she would have to have a C-section. The operation startled me – her body cut open brutally, stomach muscles sliced through; the womb lifted out so the surgeon could cut into the sac. Pearly and white, a perfect space capsule, it was sliced open and then fell away, the small astronaut revealed.

If my half sister had seen the child, I think, she would never have given it away. And I did see the child, yet I let it all go forward: in minutes the tiny infant was handed irrevocably into strangers' arms.

I know the girl will imagine, as she grows up, how it must have been – think of her lost mother, the woman with the scar on her stomach through which she once emerged into the light. I would like to find the girl, to tell her what she looked like, wrinkled, her face crumpled, but beautiful nonetheless, as she was lifted up – as she cried, bloody, and was not handed to her mother. But I cannot; with the adoption, even my sister was legally barred from her, and I, of course, have no claim on her at all.

It's hard to explain how it happened, but seeing the child's birth changed me almost by happenstance, the way a stranger's casual comment can reveal you. Ever since, I've wanted a child of my own, perhaps to make up for the one I lost that day – a child that was not mine, and yet was mine somehow. When I met Ilan, I knew he would be the one to give her back to me; the child I would someday have would be his.

A few weeks after we become engaged, Ilan says, 'I want to show you something.' He leads me into our bedroom.

On the bed, a white wedding dress lies. The bodice is silk; the skirt, minutely beaded, is so voluminous it covers half the duvet.

'I love it,' I say.

'It was my mother's. My father gave it to me to give to you.'

'It's very nice of him.' I try to sound enthusiastic, but I am worried. It seems tiny, not quite my size.

'It shows how much he likes you. As soon as I told him we were engaged, he said, "That's the girl for you." Will you try it on?'

I slip off my sundress and step into the wedding dress's skirt, carefully pulling it up to my waist. The length is right; the lush fabric of the skirt surrounds me and skims the floor. My sandals disappear underneath. I look down and imagine myself the ballerina on the music box, the bride on the wedding cake.

'Can you zip me?' I ask as I draw the thin white straps of the dress's corset up over my shoulders.

He pulls the zipper up, but it catches. I suck in my stomach. In fits and starts, he wrenches it closed. My breasts fit the décolletage but my stomach buckles the thin silk; the tight dress creates a roll of fat at my waist.

'So you'll lose a little weight,' Ilan remarks.

'This weight I can't lose. I've tried for years. Couldn't we have it altered?'

'Come on, Maya, it's just five pounds.'

'Look, will you unzip me? I can't breathe.' But he doesn't, still appraising my body in the dress.

'We can get a different one,' he offers.

'I'd like to wear it if I can.'

'But you say it's impossible.'

'I'll try again. Maybe I can lose it. Can you please unzip me?'

Finally he does.

In the weeks that follow, I try so hard to flatten my stomach, but I can't. Despite dieting, despite an obsessive regimen of yoga and sit-ups, the fat remains. My arms shrink, and my face narrows so my cheekbones rise out of it. Even my back gets thinner, my spine's nubby bones more prominent – but the fat around my waist is undiminished by an ounce.

I decide to resort to plastic surgery. I call a doctor the magazine recently touted, and learn I can afford it. It will cost almost exactly what I am due to be paid by the magazine for an interview with a celebrity couple who have moved together to Siberia – literally, Siberia.

'You don't have to do that,' Ilan remarks when I tell him.

'I want to,' I reply. 'It's harmless and I can afford it. So I'm going to.'

On my first visit, the doctor takes 'before' photographs in front of a black curtain. He is silver-haired but young-looking and very handsome. I stand before him wearing thin paper panties he provides, and for a moment he could be a pornographer. The click of the flash arouses me.

'There's no need for you to have this surgery,' he tells me.

'I might not need it, but I want it.'

'If you insist, there is fat that can be removed, but it's really not worth it.' He shows me the part of my belly he will flatten, the part that will still curve.

'I want to do it,' I repeat, and he says he will.

At our next appointment, I am scheduled to have the surgery. The area of my body from which fat is to be removed is carefully circled by the doctor with a black marker. Then I am told to lie down on a gurney. My mouth is dry and bothered; I have been forbidden to drink water for hours beforehand. I chew ice and wait for the surgeon.

I realize I find the idea of the surgery disturbingly erotic: it is a sleep in which I will be touched without consent, from which no one will awaken me until they are ready, within which I will never really know, except from later evidence, what occurred. The perfect sleep beyond mortal sleep, the perfect trust of surrendering even the ability to be roused by noise or speech. I would not even wake in a fire.

Ilan, wearing a green mask and gown, holds my hand as the anesthesia is administered. He insisted on being here, and eventually the doctor assented. The lights shine above me so brightly, in their metal cups, that it is hard for me to see. My only link to the world is Ilan's hand.

As I begin to go under, it flashes to me that it is as if he were watching me give birth, the same encouraging grasp. That is the last thought I have before I am suddenly gone.

My body has never really been my own, I have not wanted it – not since I was eighteen when occasionally, rowing, it pleased me to be in it and alive. For the past two years, ever since we met, it has been Ilan's – he who can reach down with his hand, his tongue, and make me shudder. For an hour now it is the surgeon's, and that has been my only infidelity in all this time.

The surgeon – so I am told later – makes a small incision through my belly button. Through the cut, he inserts a metal tube into my abdomen, to create a series of small canals in a fan shape; through these canals, he sucks out the fat there. Then he makes a second incision, just above my pubic hair, and inserts the tube again, pushing it upward to create another set of canals, in another fan shape, that crosshatch the first set. Through this second set of canals, fat is again sucked out. And then the operation is over.

'You had good fat,' the doctor tells me when I awaken. The nurse is holding a basin, waiting for me to throw up, but I don't; I feel good. I feel wonderful, actually. Except that I powerfully need to sleep.

'Your fat came out nicely,' the doctor continues. 'Some people's fat is like cottage cheese.'

I smile. Whether my fat was good or bad, I know I am better off without it. Now I am the girl Ilan wanted, am I not? I fit the dress, the ring, the wedding, the life that will follow.

Afterward I wear a tight girdle for a few weeks, as I have been instructed to do. All my body has to do is heal in time for the wedding, and it does heal.

Flowers of blood soak through the girdle in the first few days, then transform into yellow and purple bruises, and then the bruises fade. They heal into invisibility with a regularity that moves me – as if, rather than being a biological process, it is my body saying it wants to live. As if it believes in my life more than I do.

The scars the surgery leaves are small, perhaps an eighth of an inch long. The one from the incision in my belly button is impossible to see, lost in the tiny creases. But the one from the incision above my pubic hair is still dark red.

It is at eye level for Ilan when he goes down on me, and for a while, as he tongues me, he will touch it. It is a mark that will never leave me. At most it will fade, but I will always know it's there. In some sense, it is his mark, and I will bear it forever.

The surgery does not change my life, as perhaps in the back of my mind I hoped it would. I am not even sure, though, what I was hoping for – that it would make me so beautiful that I could be enough? That once it was accomplished, our bargain might somehow be broken, taken back?

Whatever I had hoped, it was too much. The surgery does not change me. But it does, at least, change my body. I feel the change settling in, week after week; I feel the skin shrinking over the spaces the surgery left.

That January, six weeks after the operation, I slip into Ilan's mother's dress again. I shift my breasts into the place where her breasts were, and lean over to rearrange them. I pull the dress to my waist, and all at once I am lost in the same pouf of skirt, the same soft mound of hilly satin in which she once walked.

Ilan zips the bodice up in a single quick motion. Around the dress's waist, there is room where I used to stretch it. I live in it very comfortably now, the silk falling slack over my newly flattened stomach.

I look down nervously, as if the flowers of blood that once soaked through the ugly girdle's mesh will somehow soak, too, through this glossy silk. But it is only my imagination. You would never know from the outside that I was not born this way, born to fit into a dress like this.

In the mirror one cannot – Ilan has to say it – help but think of a princess.

An announcement to be submitted to the *Times*, from which you might have believed that happiness was our birthright, is drafted at my mother's insistence, and photographs are taken to accompany it. We are to be married in April, in a Newport mansion with a lawn that leads down to the sea.

The night before we marry, I have a dream. I am underwater, just beneath the surface of a running river that would carry me away were it not for the crooked black tree branch I hold. The branch extends toward me through the water, like a hand reaching down.

The surge of the blue-green water is strong and unrelenting, and my hold on the branch is uncertain, slippery. I should be moving along it hand over hand, like a child twisting in the air, legs trailing, across the span of a jungle gym. I should be closing in on the shore, moving into the shallower water, so that I can break the water's surface and take a breath.

But I am not, I cannot move forward at all. My hand cannot even fully get purchase on the branch's mossy skin. So rather than getting closer to the riverbank, I only slide farther out along the branch's length, deeper into the water.

Underwater, I do not even hear the crack of the breaking branch. All at once I lose my grip, and I only hear the water rushing. I only feel it move my body wherever I am destined to go. The water engulfs me, and as I drown, I feel at peace. I do not bolt awake, the prospect of my own death does not jolt me into the waking world.

The truth is that I am comfortable, drowning.

On the day of the wedding, my parents pretend to get along with each other, albeit a little icily. My six half sisters are my bridesmaids, wearing light pink sleeveless dresses and carrying identical pink flowers – a row of lovely blondes that I, with my shock of red hair, interrupt. In the wedding photos, later, I look like the changeling I know I am.

Ilan's father is also his best man, which moves me – his father is so close to him, he has superseded any mere friend. Ilan has trouble coming up with groomsmen, but my four half brothers are happy to fill the gap. They flank him, in their tuxedos, as if they were his brothers too.

It occurs to me that, like me, Ilan has never had many friends; even before we met, both of us had so few. I lost touch with my few high school friends when I drew apart from my family and our town, lost touch with my college roommates when I abruptly left school. As for Ilan, he has many acquaintances – and a few glancing, slight friendships – simply because he's lived in the city all his life, attended the same private school, on the same street as his family's apartment, for twelve years. But none of his friendships are close.

He is too solitary and difficult, too strong-willed for that; his closer friendships typically ended in a disagreement he couldn't forgive, and after a while I think he stopped having them. Now he has only me – and his father.

It looks like a beautiful wedding but the core that is real is very small. It should be just the two of us, standing in a room somewhere. Instead there are two hundred people assembled, first in a hall and later in a ballroom. We marry before all of our parents' friends, having invited only a few of our own – but with my many half brothers and sisters to toast us, perhaps no one notices.

The odd service is alternately Jewish and Christian – at Ilan's father's and my parents' requests, respectively – a pastiche I was surprised everyone agreed to.

At some point, a glass breaks without cuts or blood. At some point, one of my half sisters reads: 'Love bears all. It believes all. It hopes all. It endures all.' It is not this, it is not that. I cannot remember the rest.

I remember thinking at the time, I don't know what love does, but I know what it is. It is this.

And afterward, I remember selecting in my mind only part of what my half sister said, as if certain words applied, and others did not. 'Love bears all, it endures all' – that is what I remember later.

As we are about to say our vows, Ilan's father produces a wedding ring and hands it to Ilan. 'My wife's,' he whispers to me. I almost shake my head no. There was a plastic band at rehearsal and Ilan never mentioned this.

It surprises me, this extraordinary thing. Ilan's mother's dress, her ring – her lost wedding, why has it come to us? I want to return the ring, and say to Ilan's father: 'Take another wife, you're not yet dead.' But there is no time and I don't have the heart.

I smile at Ilan's father; I hope he has not seen me wince; and I hold out my hand. Next to my yellow diamond, Ilan slides on my golden ring – and then I slide on his, and then it is done.

On our honeymoon, Ilan and I are alone in Italy – a country where he speaks the language and I do not. I begin to think, after a while, that this is why he chose it.

He does everything for me, solicitous. Our hotel rooms are filled with rose petals, and we are greeted, always, with chilled champagne. Yet every time he speaks to a pretty woman, I believe it is starting; now it will all begin.

There are several women I remember even now – as if I, not he, had been the one who wanted them. There is one with shining black eyes and a small backpack she won't take off, even sitting at the bar of the restaurant where we meet her – a woman who drinks all night next to us, smiling at Ilan more and more frequently, the more she drinks. And there is another at a museum, a blonde whose breasts shift in her sleeveless top as she moves, who wears a sweeping skirt that trails behind her almost like a bride's train. She lingers near an abstract painting that Ilan and I are looking at too – the painting delights her, and she delights Ilan, I can tell.

The suspense as to when it will all begin seems to make more acute the pleasure of the museums, the cafés, the countryside, of every moment – of the sex especially. We are obscene in bed in the Rome hotel. I ride Ilan remorselessly. He thumbs my breasts harshly, until it is too much and I tell him to stop. He presses me up against walls and doors, and he takes me; I am taken.

The intensity of his gaze is purer than usual, and he often keeps eye contact with me during sex, from beginning to end.

Once I start to describe to him the way he looks. 'You have three different expressions,' I begin.

'Don't, you'll make me self-conscious.'

I keep my thoughts to myself.

He wants to watch me, too, but he never describes to me how I look to him, except to say that I am beautiful. I have difficulty, at first, coming with my eyes open, but I learn to do it. The first time I look into his eyes and no longer care how my face contorts, I know I am sexually free, he has freed me.

He wants us to be visible from the hotel window sometimes, pushing aside the curtains so our bodies can, from the correct angle, clearly be seen. I protest at first but eventually he convinces me to forget that people can watch us, and I simply give in to him. Let them watch us, he entreats. They are strangers.

We travel to the coast and spend days on the beach. I become tan but I refuse to take off my bikini top, as many of the European women do. At our hotel, Ilan touches the lines around the still-white parts of my breasts as if they were markings of what is forbidden. He licks the line that separates white from tan, and he watches me as I watch him do so.

All this time, I almost enjoy the suspense, the

waiting to know which woman it will be. Part of me waits in dread; part, in anticipation.

In the end, though, nothing happens with any of the women to whom Ilan speaks, or whom he carefully surveils, in Italy. He watches them, yes, but in the end, he does not act. His eyes move over them and move on, like the beams of headlights playing over buildings as the car passes.

It is a time in my life I would love to relive, to replay over again and again like a videotape – with the knowledge that every threat of infidelity is false; each woman we meet will drop out of our lives forever. It is only me, for now, whom Ilan will be inside, and for now I will be the only one inside him.

When I climb the steps to board the plane that will bring us home – a sleek tourist in expensive sunglasses in a beautiful city where I have been happy – I know I can keep this time against all the time to come, a block of memory I can shore up against eternity, secrete against loss. I know this trip is both a gift and a shield against what will happen to me. And I know, too, that this is the way Ilan planned it to be.

Shortly after we return from Italy, we are to travel again, this time to Las Vegas for the weekend. I have never been there before.

Ilan has an assignment to write about the dancers

and strippers: where they come from, how much they make, and, of greatest interest to his readers, how to date one. Ilan, of course, will imply that they often date their patrons. We will never discuss it, but somehow I will be the one who ends up writing most of the article, and this is one reason, I believe, that he has taken me along.

But there is also another purpose for the trip: Las Vegas is to be the scene of our first debauch. There, where everything is legal, we will be safe. We will go far, but on a leash. The two plane trips will separate our New York lives from this experiment. Afterward, we will keep the memory separate from us, in a little compartment as tightly sealed as a souvenir snow globe.

It is a late-night flight. We rise above the lights of the city in darkness. In the row behind us, a child shrieks with complaint as the plane banks sharply, as it whirs and shakes.

I am calm. Takeoff used to make my palms sweat. I used to have a song I sang to myself silently as a ritual, as if it were a prayer to ensure all would go well. But that is not the case anymore, not when I am with Ilan. I no longer worry about dying in planes as long as I will die with him.

We are in first class, courtesy of Ilan's father. After takeoff the passengers around us, mostly business-people, begin one by one to tip their seats back and click their lights off to sleep. Even the child behind us burbles, chirps, then quiets.

Soon our bank of two seats provides the only halo of light in the section, and the stewardess attends only to us. Ilan starts drinking as soon as liquor is available.

'Will you have a drink?' he asks me.

'No.' I shake my head. I want to be fully aware when it all begins.

'You're so tight, let me feel your shoulders,' Ilan coaxes me. I relax a bit to his touch.

'This is a lark, a game,' he says quietly. 'We have to treat it that way or we'll never get through it. Have a drink,' he urges me again.

Then he wets his finger in his own drink and passes it over my lips, even as turbulence shakes us. It does not fail to arouse me.

Ilan flicks off the overhead light. First class is entirely dark now, except for the small emergency lights that run along the floor. He wets his finger in his drink again, and this time he reaches below the blue blanket in my lap.

Even in the darkness, I feel uneasy. I sense the sleeping passengers around us, I hear the small breaths of the sleeping child.

'Look at me,' Ilan whispers. 'Concentrate on me.' But I can barely see him in the darkness.

Against instructions, I shut my eyes. Quickly his

fingers are inside me and then, a moment later, in my mouth. I bite down on them. They are wet with gin, with my saliva and arousal. Then I feel them inside me again, over and over – until I am almost exhausted past coming with the ache inside, with the effort of maintaining the silence I would so like to break with a cry.

It takes a long time but finally, soundlessly, I come for him.

By the time we arrive, I have had the drink Ilan insisted upon, and three more, and I feel more ebullient than afraid. I rarely drink, so by now I am dizzy. Getting off the plane, I walk unsteadily and Ilan must hold my arm; he carries both of our bags over his shoulder.

We drive in from the airport in our spotless rental car and stop at the hotel Ilan has chosen. It is demeaning and embarrassing, but also tremendously exciting, at every step. To check into the hotel knowing what we are planning to do; to have our luggage taken from us in the lobby; to leave without even seeing our room. To drive with Ilan to find the nearby neoned strip bar that I dread, and for which I long. And to listen to him ask there for the VIP room, where we can be alone with the stripper. I am helplessly aroused by it all, even as it mortifies me.

I feel grateful to Ilan for ensuring I would be drunk; otherwise the embarrassment might have been too much. As it is, I can sit back slightly, in this heady state, and watch myself do whatever he asks.

As he walks me to the VIP room, he cups my breasts from behind so that anyone can see. I do not fight his hands, don't even try to brush them away. I feel so detached, so remote, as he touches me. It is almost as if he were touching some other woman as I watch.

The VIP room is small and two bouncers linger in the background. Their presence does not worry me. If they watch us, I think, what can it matter? Like the strangers who might have seen us in the window of the Rome hotel, they will simply have an image in their minds that happens to coincide with my body. And, as Ilan has said, why should that matter to me?

I am demure in a black dress. The blonde stripper is topless, trashy and alluring, in a gold lamé thong. The skin pulls taut over her implants; her breasts seem to float, riding high over her bony rib cage. Music begins, and she begins dancing.

'Your wife's so pretty,' the stripper says to Ilan in a southern accent.

'She is, isn't she?'

'Open your mouth for me,' she tells him. 'Open wide.'

He does as she asks, and she puts her nipple inside his mouth. She must be able to feel his

67

breath, I realize – and still his lips do not touch her at all, as he knows they cannot: the rules are clearly posted on the wall.

She keeps her nipple almost immobile as she grinds against him. Still abiding by the rules, still without his lips touching it, Ilan smiles.

As another song begins, she pulls away from him and leans over to kiss me. I am surprised – I assumed contact was forbidden for me, too – but I kiss her back. It is very much like kissing a man except her lips are smaller, softer, her tongue less insistent. Taller than I am, almost six feet in her stilettos, she cranes to kiss me just as a man would crane.

She kisses me again. And she opens my dress – in front of the bouncers, I realize, excited and ashamed: right in front of them – revealing my breasts as if I were a stripper too.

She touches my breasts, soft, imperfect, and at her invitation, I touch hers, hard and perfect, and Ilan leans back a little to have the right frame for the picture he sees.

Then she caresses me for a few more minutes, kissing me with a lovely, feigned passion, fake and theatrical and yet somehow moving for all that. If I once wondered what men saw in this, now I see it clearly – that it is only a performance does not make it worse; it makes it better. I am disturbed to see why Ilan wants it, what he sees in it, even as I am glad to know him this way.

As we kiss I feel the tip of the stripper's tongue probe my lips and I realize it is a frisson of her technique, a small embellishment. I open my lips to her a little, to let her play. This must be what men want too: to push the girl beyond her job; to seem to take from her some intimate thing she has withheld. I feel it myself, the wanting; feel her lips on mine and what they mean: how they could go further, how much I would like it.

The song ends and Ilan announces, 'It's time for us to go.'

'You're very good,' he says to the stripper.

'Come back and we'll do a little more next time,' she promises. I am afraid of the 'more' but I want to know, too, what it would be.

'Can I touch you next time?' Ilan asks her in a whisper.

'May-be,' she lilts. 'You'll just have to see.'

Surreptitiously, she hands Ilan her calling card. He pays her in cash, and I notice that he tips well above the quoted rate. For the magazine, he writes down what he has spent.

In the parking lot, he hands me the card. It reads 'Lily – Professional Dancer and Entertainer' and gives a cell phone number. I wonder if in addition to being a stripper, she is also a prostitute.

On impulse I throw the card away in a trash can. While I can tell it annoys Ilan, he makes a show of not minding.

'Our friend Lily was pretty good, don't you think?' he comments. 'But I'm sure there are better.'

We return to our hotel and order room service. Ravenous, we order decadently – for me, French toast with syrup, strawberries, a silver boat of cream; for Ilan, a thick steak. We bring our trays to bed. Wolfing down the food, I feel callous – maybe I am callous.

Later Ilan goes out to 'interview' other strippers for his article. I know – I can visualize now – what it will be like, how close he will be to them and how they will invite him to get closer, to gradually take more and more as he gradually pays more and more.

This time, though, he doesn't ask me to accompany him. He says it will be too dangerous; he is going to the more low-rent clubs. Instead, he says, he'll take notes, tell me all about it later.

When he leaves, I think of him stopping at boarded-up buildings on the road that lies next to the glittery Strip like the paler, empty skin a glinting reptile has cast off. I think of him going alone to places he did not want to take me.

I lie alone and awake in our vast bed at the hotel for several hours, wondering if I am going to cry but feeling no impulse to do so.

When we return to the city, Ilan begins the Vegas article himself, but soon we fall into our old college pattern. One afternoon, he goes out to visit the magazine's offices for an editorial meeting, and I begin to tinker with the story on his laptop – adding anecdotes; sharpening and ironizing the descriptions of the dancer, of our hotel.

'What is this?' he demands when he returns, and sees what I have done.

'Some edits.'

'You think I can't write this myself?'

'Of course I do. I just thought it would be faster this way – like in college,' I dare to remind him.

'I want to do it myself. Take out what you added.'

I remove it all, but even then I know how this will end. Later that night, when he is almost in tears with frustration, I take over again, and he contents himself with working on something else. I put back much of what he has forced me to remove, and he says nothing when the old material reappears in the final draft I show him.

He submits the piece, and his father loves it, and Ilan takes credit. But on the phone with his father, accepting the compliments, he looks at me warily, as if I am somehow a threat to him now.

A few weeks later, Ilan shows me an ad he has placed in the *Village Voice*:

A LOVE AFFAIR IN A DAY. My wife and I will meet you, love you, and leave you forever. We won't betray your secrets. We won't even know each other's names. She's beautiful, if it matters. You must be 5'9", 130, a redhead – like her. You won't regret it.

Beneath the ad, there is a voice mailbox number. Noticing the *Voice*'s ad submission deadlines, set off in a black box near the ad, I realize that Ilan must have been drafting the ad at the same time I was writing his Vegas article – as if this were his vocation now, his life's work. The thought scares me.

The ad itself scares me a little too. It makes me wonder if he wants me in multiples because he loves me so much, or so little. Was there some way that by myself, I could have been enough – a path, but I couldn't find it? Isn't there some way we can go on as we have been – perhaps just with strippers, going only as far as we went last time? I have been so happy, and I am so afraid of losing that feeling. Perhaps I should plead with him to change his mind.

Thinking about it more carefully, though, I decide to keep quiet. I know how serious this promise is to him; after all, our marriage is predicated on it. And one thing about the ad did strangely reassure me: at least if the women look just like me, they cannot be that much prettier.

'You won't regret it,' I murmur to myself, parroting Ilan's ad.

*   *   *

Ilan arranges to meet each of the women who leave a message in response to the ad – providing the address of a bar or museum, and telling her when he'll be there.

I am always there too, a few yards away, with my red hair concealed under a cap. The women never seem to notice me – perhaps because Ilan has assured them beforehand that he will be alone.

If Ilan doesn't find a woman attractive, he leaves before she even knows he's there, subtly motioning for me to leave with him. Since the women are redheads, they are always simple to pick out. So if he does not want her, he simply walks away.

But if he does want the woman, if he thinks her pretty, he'll introduce himself, giving a false name, and linger to talk with her, test her. I stay to watch, judging from afar. If we are in a museum, I'll appear to be intent on a sculpture; if it is a bar, I'll pretend to read a book as I sip my drink. I eavesdrop, picking up as much of their conversation as I can.

As I watch, I have the same feeling I did when I came upon Ilan with that first woman in the summerhouse: I'm a ghost now. I am dead and this is the first woman he has met whom he really likes, after he has mourned me. I like being a ghost. It is so much easier than being alive.

Always, Ilan only considers women for whom this will be a scary departure, a first time. The 'alternative-lifestyle' ones can go to hell, he says, with their shoulder tattoos, their swinging and the accompanying silly jargon. He wants the straight, the even ones. The good, the sweet ones. The girls like me are the ones he likes, he confesses – the ones where you would never think, to look at them, that they would even consider this. They are the ones Ilan wants, the ones he waits for.

I have to admit, it is so sexy – all these slender, pretty women, often with husbands who don't know. We will take them home, I imagine, and they will open for us like clocks, their delicate inner workings revealed. We will see their pieces, see inside.

It is lovely for Ilan to choose among the women; he does not want it to stop. He takes a long time to decide on the first one. There are several women I approve, but he finds an eleventh-hour reason to reject each of them.

'The first one has to be perfect,' he explains.

Finally, though, he does choose a woman, and he sets a date, in mid-December. The name she has given us is Rebecca, but I know it is probably false, like the names we have given her, John and Jane.

On the night he has chosen, I wait for them in the loft. I draw the curtains over its huge windows in preparation. In the darkness the apartment feels smaller and closer. I cannot remember when my heart has raced like this before – except when it did so for Ilan. Now, again, my heart pounds as if it is gulping blood.

But as nervous as I am, I am almost glad it is finally happening: since we married, this promise has been with me like my marriage vow itself, like the ring I wear.

Finally the key turns in the lock and they enter. He places a bottle of champagne on the sideboard and helps her with her coat.

I have approved her, have been part of choosing her, but it is difficult actually to have her here, with Ilan lifting her coat from her shoulders – as he always does for me.

Rebecca is a tomboy of a woman, incredibly lithe – once upon a time a dancer, she has told Ilan. Though she is my height and weight, as Ilan's ad ensured, she is smaller than I, with tiny wrists and little hands, so thin-skinned their blue veins are visible. She is pretty but not beautiful, and that is how I prefer it. If she were beautiful, and I were to watch him with her, I might have to cry.

She wears a dark evening dress cut high at the neck. I am in a T-shirt and skirt, as if this weren't particularly important, as if we do this all the time.

She strides up to me confidently and stands there, considering me. Ilan introduces us, and for a second she takes my hand. We say hello quietly.

'Would you like a drink?' she asks me as she deftly uncorks the bottle of champagne. It feels strangely presumptuous: shouldn't Ilan have been the one to open it? Then I realize we are outside etiquette here, outside society and the rules of its life.

'You go ahead,' I say, and she does – taking a glass from the sideboard, she fills it and sips it in front of me.

'It's really good,' she says.

'No thanks.' I want and need to do this cold sober; I need it to be different from Las Vegas.

Ilan is visibly restless, intuiting that I may change my mind – in a moment I could dash out and our marriage could be over. I can feel his fear. It somehow makes me more comfortable that he too is afraid.

'Really, have some champagne,' Rebecca urges me. She must feel it too, my urge to bolt like a spooked colt. Ilan stays back, watching.

'No thanks,' I repeat stiffly.

Putting her drink down, she shoves me a little, slipping to the side of me and shouldering me a bit. 'Cut it out,' she says. 'Why are you making it so hard?'

I shove her back playfully. '*You* cut it out.'

She shoves me again, but this time not quite so hard. It recalls to me the rough-and-tumble of childhood, where sexuality was always just underneath, the force that drove the horseplay, the clambering and climbing.

I think suddenly of all the girls who touched me then, with never even a question in their touch, and I think of how, when boys and later men had touched me, there was always a question, a proposition, a dare. Who drew that line for me – the line between the two kinds of touch? And can I cross it now?

Ilan seems worried, about to say something. But he steps farther back from us, just when I think he may step in. Leaning against the sideboard, he waits.

Rebecca shoves me once more. And then she has permission to kiss me and knows it, and she kisses me hard.

We kiss over and over, and I lead her to the writing room. Ilan and I have agreed that everything with the women will happen in this room, the one I dream will be a child's someday – never in our bedroom.

Soon she has me lying on the bed there. As I lower my head to the pillow, a sweet dizziness rushes in, a feeling that seems to lift off of me like fizz. A giddiness, as if I have been drinking after all.

It's in me, I know that from her first rough touch. I can be with her, I can want to. I am crossing the line and as I cross it, it disappears, until it is as if it never existed at all. I am going to like what I've been required to do, and for once, not merely because I have been required to do it.

Rebecca slips my clothes off in a moment and shimmies down the bed until her mouth is at my waist.

I open to her as I would to a man – meaning, I suppose, as I would to Ilan, for the sex with the two boys who preceded him he has long ago erased.

It is not so very different to have her lick me – though I twist to the thrill of the smaller tongue, its finer point. But I know what is expected of me – I must do to her what she is doing to me – and I fear it.

It will have to be a giving over, I tell myself; I will have to give myself over to this, without my second-guessing mind. Still, my heart is rampantly beating as if it will never slow.

The body that scares me so much is just like my own, I think to myself. Why should I fear it? This should be easy for me; I ought to know the very touch that is likely to prostrate, to disarm.

As she licks me, I become wet. She arouses me, and thinking about licking her arouses me as well. The fear itself, I realize, makes me wet.

I fold my tongue into a U in my mouth, thinking of what I soon must do to her – as I squirm beneath her tongue, and beneath her touch.

I switch places with her. I have to start instantly or I'll never start at all – and I do start.

It feels like licking a wound when it is still soft, still touchy and tender – with that much tentativeness – licking the red soft cut that is exposed, reinflicted as the scab is torn off. I fall in love with that softness in a moment; there is nothing so soft, I realize, on a man.

I begin to lick her harder, to recognize in her flinches my own. And as I flick and tongue and rub Rebecca, I learn for the first time what Ilan must see when he goes down on me: she is splayed above me, small and thin but in a way also huge and curved – hilly as a Botero sculpture, and vulnerable as it is possible to be. Writhing in pain and pleasure, she is powerful and lost, as if a force is working its way through her. It is an exorcism, an imbuement, a leave-taking, an arrival.

With my hands on her thighs, I feel the strong muscles there flex as she bicycles her feet into the mattress, as agitated as she is aroused.

For a second I raise my head to look at Ilan, like a thirsty animal interrupted drinking. I smile and in my smile there is a clear message: 'You were not sure if I could do this, but I have.'

Taking my look as an invitation, he moves in to kiss Rebecca. It surprises me that he is kissing her first – not kissing me, as I thought he would, to reassure me. For an instant it galls me to see it, but then he turns to me and kisses me instead, and again I'm in his thrall.

Rebecca slips down between my legs again, and in a moment Ilan is on my breasts, tonguing them as she licks my clitoris. It is too much for me, I come even though I don't want to – even though I do not want to give that last thing up yet, not now. I would prefer to keep watching this, to keep myself apart from it for now. But I can't – not anymore.

I give myself up to it, lose myself in it. I know I look as Rebecca just looked to me, and I do not mind it. I want her and I want him. I feel shame and do not care.

I come hard, the orgasm is like a wind tearing me away from myself. It has a kick, a backlash. It leaves me coughing with tears. I hate myself, but I cannot stop coming, and in a way I love it too.

Then Ilan watches as I make Rebecca come. He helps me draw her closer and, toward the end, bring her over the edge. It takes me a long time, I am still inexpert – but he helps me only a little. He kisses her but he leaves it to me to touch her, and then he moves away from us, to watch us together. He does not come, himself, while she is there.

As she is leaving, Rebecca raises her eyebrows at us and says, 'I had a great time. Would you be interested in a second date?'

But Ilan says quickly, 'We have a rule that we don't see anyone twice.'

'I understand,' she says, looking at us both. 'I'm sure it's hard enough.'

'It's fine,' Ilan says coolly.

'Good night, then.' Rebecca looks embarrassed to have suggested the strain this must put on our marriage. She slips out, quietly shutting the door.

Once she has left, Ilan begins to touch me, and soon he enters me. I am still wet but my arousal feels compromised, for I know Rebecca, not Ilan, made me that way. Being with him feels fraught, strange, but only for a moment; in a moment, it feels normal again. Sex with her was a dream, and sex with him is my life – at least, that is what I tell myself.

Afterward we lie in bed for a while. In pajamas, we drink tea Ilan has made.

I sit calmly beside him, with my toes under his thighs on the couch, the way we used to sit at school. And I realize, all at once, that we've done this, it's over, and I have not left him. Yet I am still unsure whether I want this, at least a little, or whether only he does; whether I like it or only he does. Whether it is an acquired taste he has truly taught me, or only a way in which I am trying to resemble him.

'You've never come that way before,' Ilan says.

'I didn't want to,' I admit.

'But you liked it?'

'It was very . . . intense.'

'That's the way I like it. It's something that's taken from you, you don't give it. It's going to happen whether you like it or not.'

'It was so surreal. That feeling, having it for the first time, the feeling that I couldn't control it, and having it with her – and then she leaves, we never see each other again.'

'That was the idea.'

Yet I know, afterward, that I will not be able to separate this from my life as easily as he can. There will never be a clear blue day for me, once I decide that I like this, that I really can do it; I know that.

But who said I wanted a clear blue day? Instead perhaps I want a throatful of tears. Perhaps I want to take coming as Ilan takes it, almost without pleasure – like a straight shot of alcohol tossed back without taste, yet with a greater, quicker effect for all that.

After the night with Rebecca, I move uneasily but giddily into my new life. A strange mixture of relief and danger elates me. My marriage will last, I know that now, and so I am safe in at least that respect. But how will it evolve?

I cannot predict where we will go from here. All I have read is the first chapter of the story; all I know is that the story will continue, it will take us – in a reverie, inexorably – somewhere else.

Ilan sets himself the task of finding the second woman, and he is avid. Meanwhile, I work on both his writing and my own. Ilan tries to do the articles himself sometimes, but gives up in disgust.

'I don't know why the writing is so hard for me, but it is,' he complains.

'Don't worry, it's the reportage that matters,' I assure him. 'Without that there'd be no story. The writing is just translation, organization.' Secretly, though, I believe it is much more. I feel sometimes that it is the only valuable thing inside me; the only thing I have for myself alone, *as* myself alone. Everything else I have, I have because of Ilan.

Ilan's father continues to praise him for everything I submit – commenting several times on how much his writing has improved. His remarks are painful to Ilan, but he craves his father's approval enough to want simply to please him, without especially caring how it happens. And so, increasingly, Ilan makes the phone calls, visits the subjects, and then hands me his scribbled notes. We never even talk about it anymore.

Much of Ilan's time now is spent reading our ad responses. There are surprisingly many, for he has renewed the ad in the *Voice*, and placed it elsewhere, too: on the Nerve Web site, and in other newspapers. Soon he spends many of his days focusing only on this – on reading the women's letters, looking at their photos, choosing the ones to whom he will respond.

With the second woman, Cara, Ilan asks me to greet her and take her into the writing room. It is January now, about a month after our first assignation, with Rebecca.

'My husband is going to join us later,' I tell Cara.

She is a milky-skinned redhead whose freckles are muted, as if underlaid below her pale skin. I had not remembered how lovely it looked, this partial concealment.

I take Cara's coat, slipping it from her narrow shoulders: another action I have never done, I realize. I have never stood behind a woman as she shrugs off her coat, trusting me to hold what has just enveloped her. For a second, the casual eroticism of the gesture overwhelms me. She has uncloaked herself and I hold the cloak. I will choose, later, whether and when to return it to her.

I suddenly have the impulse to go further, to strip her further, but for now I refrain. I would never have thought I would be the one who wanted it faster, wanted it now; but I am, I do. With Rebecca, I feared what would happen. Now it is myself, my desire, that scares me: mine, and Ilan's, and how they will combine.

I have what I want soon enough, and I do not even have to ask. Again I have the strange feeling of being in a dream – but this time it is a dream in which I see my own desire spread out before me, made real. In the writing room, Cara slips off her beaded top. Falling, it clicks on the floor.

Then she slips her breasts out of their bra cups

and I take them in my hands, cupping them as I touch her nipples with my thumbs. Reaching behind her back, I unhook her bra and slip it off. Bared, slipping downward slightly, her breasts tremble.

Her bare feet pad on our bare floor as I walk her backward, like a dancer leading, toward the bed. She breaks away from me for a moment, but only so she can slip her skirt and panties off in a single motion, hooking them with a thumb. As she steps out of them with a graceful hop, I see that her pubic hair is also red.

Ilan watches us through a crack of the closet door – hung up there on his own desire, in stillness; watching us as if we were alone. He lets us stay awhile on the bed by ourselves, until we are used to being with each other, until I can almost forget he is there.

Then he opens the closet door slowly, so that it creaks. Cara tenses beneath me. 'It's my husband,' I reassure her.

Ilan has chosen, today, to wear a dark suit. He tells us to undress him and together we do. I slip my finger into the full knot of his tie to loosen it, its silk soft as skin. Cara wrenches his belt buckle to the side and slips his belt off in an instant. He steps out of his loafers, peels off his socks. I see the vanity, the debauchery in the scenario, but it does not stop me from wanting him, from wanting him naked as we are naked.

Soon Cara opens Ilan's shirt meticulously, button by button, and there, as always, is the chain, and she, like every fascinated woman, must touch it. She holds the tiny silver hand in her palm, then in her mouth. I begin to tear up, then, for I too have taken the metal hand into my mouth, imagining I was taking part of him that way. I did not know I would have to give up even this.

Finally she lets the chain fall from her mouth, and Ilan begins to kiss her. I slip to the corner of the bed, perching tenously there, as Ilan and Cara spread out.

He strokes her nipples. She doesn't touch him, but the way she arches her back shows she longs for this.

He moves fast with her, and soon he is inside her. Her skin is so light, it makes his look darker. And she is so ethereal, she makes him look stronger than he is. He cannot help but look as if he is overcoming her.

He hikes her legs above his shoulders to find the angle he wants, bending her into a sculpture of submission. He stretches her as far as she goes, penetrating her slowly, over and over. As he moves inside her, her cries are both loud and curt, as if they are being forced out of her.

She tells him over and over to stop, but he only tells her confidently, 'You don't really want me to.' It is a long time before he speeds his motion to bring her to climax, and when he does, she looks at him, almost astonished, as she finally loses control.

When Ilan releases her, she stands up and starts to massage her muscles, calming the backs of her thighs to keep them from shaking.

'I'm so sore,' she says to Ilan softly. 'I usually can't come during sex. Thank you.'

Ilan smiles. Then he slides over to me; I am still on the bed, frozen, watching. He kisses me and I kiss him back, and then he enters me, copying exactly the positions he used with Cara, in a way that feels almost mocking. My legs, too, dangle over his shoulders. I too am forced, through slow repetition, into pleasure.

Cara watches us together, watches Ilan make me violently come, and touches herself as she watches. Then she leaves.

Ilan and I are always alone together, at the end. There is always the sound of the door shutting. And there is always a woman who leaves us behind forever and returns to her life. I always imagine her emerging onto the street below us, into the dark, free night. And I always envy her a little, the woman leaving – while at the same time understanding that I am not the type of woman who leaves.

It hurts me, of course it does, to have seen Ilan with Cara; to have seen him enter her; to have watched him bring her all the way there, to the point where she was at his will, acting at his pleasure. But the pain is like a small knife, I learn: I can choose to take it out to cut myself, or to leave it in its drawer.

I can cut myself hard with this knife, by focusing on my image of Ilan and Cara. Or by calling up their image for just a second or two, I can cut myself just a little and gradually – as if I were peeling an apple delicately to separate its flesh from a continuous spiral of skin.

Later I even enjoy taking this imagined knife out sometimes; I enjoy thinking about, and even seeing, Ilan with another woman. Shall I be honest? It drives me to distraction.

The key is that he is between my legs, not hers, at the end. When it is all over, he chooses me and she is banished. In this way, it is almost reassuring: I have seen my worst fear, and in the end it is not real; he is still with me, still mine.

I know it is a sickness to feel this way. But there is this: I can't *feel* it as a sickness – not in a way that could convince me to leave, anyway. What I feel is only that I want Ilan, and I always, always have. I always have and I never stopped, and I never even wanted to – not until the very end, and by then it was too late.

After Rebecca and Cara, there are a few more women – all different, all the same. Redheads all in a row – reminding me oddly of my bridesmaids, that row of blondes. Women whom he is inside, while they are here. Women who stay inside me, once they leave.

As winter continues, Ilan and I fall into a routine. He will work obsessively on the reporting for one of his articles, and at the same time he will interview a few possible women, with me looking on. As he narrows the choice of women down, he will turn his notes for the article over to me so that I can 'write them up.' Then he will schedule a session with his favorite, to take place soon after his article is due, as a sort of reward.

Because Ilan's articles are often exposés, the assignations with the women usually celebrate someone else's downfall as much as they do Ilan's own success. Sometimes his joy in his subjects' defeats seems to me the worst part of him – worse than what he has me do in bed, because it is crueler.

But I wonder, sometimes, if the cruelty is all his. After all, I am his writer, his finisher, his fixer: the one who completes the assassination, who twists the knife. I am the one who chooses the phrase that captures, that hurts.

If I too feel anger, though, I never let myself know it. I tell myself I am only maintaining our life together – saving Ilan from the misery that writing is for him, allowing him to succeed. I tell myself, too, that since it is as if we are one person, it does not matter who writes the stories, in the end.

But I also realize I would never allow him to write for me, even if he offered to. I would keep back that last thing, my one talent.

It is that February, strangely, that I begin to succeed, with a series of celebrity interviews – to succeed more than I would ever have thought possible, especially since I am doing two jobs at once, fulfilling both Ilan's contract and my own. Perhaps the pressure focuses me; perhaps I am simply lucky.

It all begins when I take a risk, speculating that an actress, though single, is pregnant. I see it in what she eats and the care with which she chooses it; in her sudden success in breaking the chain-smoking habit that was so evident, in photographs of her, only months ago.

Later I find confirmation of my suspicions in the second-floor room in her house that is partially cleared, as if to be redecorated. When we walk past the room, she smiles a secret smile, and I feel in her a serene happiness, a feeling so alien to me that I cannot help recognizing it. She is like the self I imagine I could be if I were happy.

When I claim in print that the actress is pregnant, she at first issues a lukewarm denial. But a few weeks later, she replaces it with a happy announcement, explaining that she did not want the pregnancy known earlier, in case of miscarriage.

It is then that the phone starts ringing with offers for me to write for other magazines – the first I have received. I am surprised at how upset Ilan seems to be when he hears of the calls – though I assure him I would never leave his father's magazine.

He ascribes it all to a lucky guess, but I know it was more. It was the vision of a real future into which the actress was moving, one that her face betrayed.

Ilan begins to find fault with my writing then, asking for more and more rewrites on his pieces. As with the very first piece I worked on for him, he'll often erase my additions, but then later allow me to replace them word for word. I begin secretly to save different versions to delete and to revive.

One day, he says to me, 'I'll just have to start doing my own rewrites again.'

'Fine,' I tell him. But the next day, while he is out, his laptop is left open on his desk for hours, its screen glowing, and I know what that means. I take a seat, and I begin to type.

The exposé I write for him turns out to be famously nasty, for I begin the piece with an assault: all the most brutal quotes in a row. By the time one has read them, it is too late for the subject, who has been thoroughly eviscerated. Nothing the reader learns in the rest of the article could ever compensate for the damage – any more than the dead, once dead, can ever live again.

The style of the piece is so notorious that it becomes Ilan's – or, really, my – modus operandi, and he, too, begins to have some success, to garner some note in the small world of New York journalism. He, too, begins to be talked about under the gossips' breaths, at the few parties we attend. He is discreetly pointed at, and so am I.

We begin to have an image as a couple then – an image so real, it is as if each of us had a second body; as if a man and a woman who looked like us, but were not us, had somehow been born.

I have seen photographs of these new people. They are beautiful, wealthy, talented, lucky. Above all, they are happy – so happy, and so in love. He is the only one for her, she for him; as if they were made for each other.

The images' divergence from reality is so extreme, it hurts my heart.

Meanwhile, our appointments with the women continue – and with each, I am more aroused and at the same time, more disturbed.

Each evening we are to meet with one of them, Ilan puts out champagne, perhaps because it is a light drink he believes we won't regret in the morning, an evanescent one that will not leave a trace.

For my part, I put our framed photographs away in a drawer, stash away our medications, and scan the apartment for anything else, however small, that might reveal us.

One night, as I take a bottle of anxiety medication out of our medicine cabinet and hide it away, I realize I am stripping from our apartment the very type of information that helps me to understand – to see inside – the celebrities I interview. The diagnostic, the characterizing information. The medication, for instance, speaks of a looming fear, a constant discomfort that only a drug can vanquish, and raises the question of what the fear's origin might be – a question I would rather ignore.

Here, in our bare loft, we are immortal, impersonal and perfect. In life we are far from so: we are fraying; I am in pain; Ilan senses it and does nothing.

Imagining that we are on the dream platform is the only way I can tolerate the women now – endure watching their pleasure as Ilan, inside them, presses so hard that it seems as if he wants to seal his flesh to theirs.

It is the only way I can watch their closed eyes, their open mouths, as I look on with my closed mouth, my open eyes. It is the only way I can allow myself to shake with their arousal, to lose myself to this despite its dangers.

*   *   *

Soon a rising actor – already famous, about to become more so – calls the magazine and asks that I be the one to interview him. Mr Resnick is only too happy to oblige, for the actor promises an exclusive, and since his new movie comes out this month, it is an unusual coup. Ordinarily the actor would have spoken to as many magazines as possible, scored as many covers as he could.

I arrive at the actor's house, and when he ushers me in, I find we are alone. There is no publicist to accompany him and no personal assistant, and he has asked beforehand that the photographer from the magazine arrive separately, on another day. He brings coffee for both of us, and as I pour the milk that lightens mine, I begin my questioning.

'Why did you ask for me?' I begin.

'I liked your article about Marianne's pregnancy, but I hated how perceptive you were. It made me think eventually you'd find me out too.'

'Find out what?'

'I'm gay,' he tells me curtly. 'Didn't you know?'

'Not for certain.'

'Oh, you knew,' he accuses me. 'Everyone knows, don't they? They just won't say it to my face.'

'I'd heard rumors.' I dare to lie to draw him in further.

'Well, they're true,' he tells me. 'Look, you can write it, okay? But write it as a trial balloon. I'm tired of hiding, but I don't want to lose my career over it. If people are appalled, I'll just say my private life is private, like I always do. Otherwise I'll applaud you for outing me.'

And so I make a another dubious bargain, and make my name at the same time – for the story is printed, Hollywood is accepting, and the star allows me a follow-up interview, which becomes my third cover in as many months. In the follow-up interview, he talks about his lover – a younger, also semifamous actor – and the issue sells out in less than a day, then goes into a second print run.

The calls from editors come in again – offering me more money, a high title, guaranteed covers, if I will only leave. They send me flowers, ask me to lunches that I do not always decline – in a few instances I go, but keep it secret from Ilan.

I fear telling him about the lunches, since I know he will be angry that I am being courted by others. Besides, I am not seriously considering leaving the magazine. And yet it cannot be denied now: I am no longer the princess in her lonely prison tower, and he is no longer my single, saving prince.

This is when the turn happens, the change. I remember the precise day it occurred.

One Saturday in April, only a few weeks before our first wedding anniversary, I watch Ilan interview a new woman – her name is Jennifer – at the Frick. The museum has few visitors during the day, so it is easy for Ilan to talk privately to her there – and easy for him to position her near a doorway so I can overhear. I think he enjoys the idea of a seduction among works of art, as if he could as easily take home the porcelain-skinned beauty in an Ingres painting as the real woman he slowly seduces in front of it.

Jennifer gesticulates a lot, and laughs too loudly for the hushed atmosphere of the museum. She is busty, blowsy, slightly crass, overly tanned.

I tell Ilan, after we've returned home, 'I don't like her, I think she's fake.'

'I think you'd like her if you met her, actually,' he says. 'You have a lot in common.' He pauses. 'I really want this one.'

'Well, I really don't.' I am surprised he is arguing with me; I have turned down a number of women before, and he has always been apologetic about having even suggested them.

'I met her,' he objects. 'You didn't. You only saw her from far away. So you have to trust me on this one.'

He comes up behind me, places his hands on my breasts. I am immediately aroused. The more we are with other women, the more insatiable I am to be with him alone. But I push him away.

'You said I could choose them. I'm choosing. I don't want her.'

'Do it for me,' he pleads.

'I do this *all* for you. This one thing, I don't want to do. You're asking me to have sex with her, and I don't even want to touch her. She repels me.'

'You don't have to touch her.' He raises his eyebrows, and I feel myself losing again. I know I will do whatever he asks – indeed, I will love doing it; it will be, in the end, as if I had chosen it.

'If I don't have to touch her,' I tell him, 'maybe it's okay.'

The day Ilan has arranged for us to meet Jennifer, I am dressed in a white satin slip, and he blindfolds me. He ties me to a chair in the writing room, with the three silk cords pulled tight around my hands. Then he takes the wedding ring from my finger – the first time since we married that I have not worn it. He leaves to pick her up and bring her here. Silently I wait for them.

As they step inside the apartment, her trill of a laugh grates. When they enter the writing room, she gets quiet, and whispers, 'Is that her?' – as if I am damaged somehow, or sick – and it is as if I hear his nod, and then her smile.

'Do you think she's pretty?' he asks.

'Sort of. Not *so* pretty. Why did you tie her up?'

'Because I wanted to. She lets me do what I want. Are you going to be that easy?'

'Easier,' she promises.

They move to the bed and I hear the labored

breathing that I imagine they themselves, inside their arousal, are unaware of. They kiss and kiss, almost inaudibly – each kiss silent until the small slide and suck of its ending.

I hear her small kitten cries as he touches her. I can tell he wants to moan back, but he suppresses it. He won't go to that level of insult, won't be quite free with her in front of me yet.

Hearing her cries, I move through a tremendous rage like a pulsing light – vast and murderous, and it would be a blinding rage if I were not already blindfolded in this perfect dark.

Suddenly she is quiet again. 'Wait a minute,' she says to him.

I hear her walk over to me. Then I feel her finger as it draws a line under my nipples, through the thin satin.

'Too bad for you, whatever your name is,' she says. 'I have a husband at home and now I have a lover, too. But you, you have nothing. I feel sorry for you.'

She says it with such satisfaction, and Ilan does not contradict her.

'Hey, come back here,' he says to her lazily.

I hear her walk back to the bed, and then I know from the satisfied noises she makes that he is touching her. In a few moments I realize with a pang that he has gotten inside her without my knowing it. He is inside her now.

Soon I hear her come to orgasm, loud but still

kittenish, and very obviously satisfied. She is quite an actress; I can tell by her cries that she enjoys that I hear them.

Perhaps twenty minutes later – after a whispered conversation I cannot quite make out – they begin again. By now, the rage in me has started to evaporate until I am calmer, I am someplace else. Again I am the quietest girl, the stillest waiter: my most basic self.

I feel myself slowly becoming as wet as I was angry. I move through jealousy into some deeper feeling. My pain, in the end, excites me even as I suffer it. Ilan must have known, when he planned this, that it would be this way.

She's on her knees for him now, I can tell, and he is inside her, thrusting from behind. She gives a low moan every time he moves into her, hard and unchecked. Her calls rise in a false crescendo – still a display for my benefit – until again she climaxes, or pretends to.

A long moment passes. Ilan unbinds me and takes the blindfold off. I blink even though the lights are dim.

Jennifer is lying back on the bed, chest heaving, winded. On her nipples are Ilan's wedding ring and mine. Her left nipple swells around my smaller ring but Ilan's rests securely on her right nipple, as if it had been made to fit there.

Her breasts are fantastic, full and lovely and

slightly tan, and I can almost see them in the way I know Ilan did. I know how he must have felt as he slipped the rings on, as he screwed my ring slightly tighter over her nipple.

Now Ilan walks over to Jennifer, slips the rings off, and pockets them. We have married her, I think. We married this.

'You can go now,' Ilan tells her.

'That wasn't what we discussed,' she says.

'Are you listening? I'm telling you to leave.'

'It's demeaning for you to just fuck me and dismiss me. This was supposed to be foreplay. It was supposed to be a threesome. I want her' – she points at me – 'not just you.'

'I'm telling you to leave. There's nothing here for you now. Bye, Jenny. Good night.'

'Good night,' I repeat after him quietly.

Jennifer dresses sullenly. As she steps into her high heels, I think of that first angry girl at the summerhouse, indignant, leaving. I want the toss of the head that would shake her breasts a little, but it never comes.

She shrugs on her coat without Ilan there to hold it for her. He has by then gotten on the bed with me, and he is occupied in trying to convince me with his touch that the place in which we will end up, after all this, is worth all that we have done, and all that we have lost, to get there.

Ilan caresses me over and over, running his hands

gently along my back, moving his fingers tenderly over the edges of my face. Jennifer's departure is announced by a slamming door. He slips my ring back on my finger, and offers me his, but I don't accept it.

'Do I take you? I do,' he says. 'I still do. Do you take me?'

I say nothing. I want to say no. After a moment, he slips the ring on his own finger.

'Cry, then,' he orders me, annoyed. 'I know you want to.'

I start to cry.

The next afternoon I am trying to write up another interview at the apartment. Again I feel confident it will be a cover story, especially since I believe that Mr Resnick, like Ilan, must know of the offers that have come in, attempting to lure me away. But I can't work, I can't write it; I am in pain.

I play with my wedding ring, which I had put back on but now remove again, working it past my fingertip and then holding it in my palm. Eventually I slip it back into place and resume typing, but it still bothers me. Loose on my finger – it was never properly fitted for me – it moves up and down slightly as my hands move, traversing the span between my knuckle and the end of my fingers' fork: that small space within which it can wander, but which it can never leave.

The princess in her locked castle, I think to myself bitterly, enchanted by the golden ring she must always wear.

It does not help my mood that the celebrity about whom I am writing left her husband because he cheated on her. I know her type: she is that admirable kind of woman who deserves better and is well aware of it. Indeed, she is already dating someone else, a younger musician who is crazy about her, she says. I noticed, when she gave me a tour of her house, that he had left no clothing in her closets, and her toothbrush still leaned solo in its holder. But I also knew that if he didn't move in eventually, she would leave him, too.

Who are these women, I wonder, and what is the source of their confidence? How is it that they can leave?

Unable to write a word more, I languish on an upholstered chair, cradling my laptop.

Near me Ilan is busily typing away, bent over his own laptop, which sits on the wooden desk where he works. I believe his writing – he is working, finally, on one of his own articles – is a peace offering of sorts, an admission that he hurt me on the night with Jennifer, that he has burdened me too heavily by asking me to write all his pieces, as well as my own. But it feels like too little, too late.

I imagine leaving him but immediately I am flooded with sadness; I understand just how hard it would be, how painful to bear. I imagine handing him a plate of fishhooks with my blood on them – a silver platter of bloody metal and caught on it, scraps of ripped-up skin. I imagine saying to him, 'Here, I've finally torn you out.' Saying: 'I'm willing to bleed to leave you. It is right, finally, that I leave you.'

'Can we please stop?' I ask him. I blurt it out. I wanted never to challenge him. But I can't help it.

'Stop what?'

'You know what.'

'I thought we talked about this a long time ago. We went through this. We decided it together.'

'But I didn't think it would be like *this*. I feel like I'm losing myself. Like I don't even have a self, I just do what you tell me.'

'Which excites you.' He raises his eyebrows at me, smug.

'We shouldn't have done the thing with Jennifer. You shouldn't have made me do it.'

'You seemed to like it at the time. I see you with these women, Maya. You pretend it's for me but I know you like it. It makes me jealous how much you like it, but I still let you do it. Isn't it exciting, to have new desires – to change? That's why we're alive, isn't it?'

He kicks his feet up on the table and leans back casually as he quizzes me.

103

'I tried to change,' he tells me, 'and I couldn't – I'm not as lucky as you. You're the one who turned into the famous writer. I'm still toiling here. You're the one who learned that you like women – that you *love* them. I'm the known quantity, Maya, and you're the one who's interesting. Let me show you who you are. Experiment with me a little. I want to try something else with you.'

'What?'

'Trust me.'

'I trusted you before and you brought home a woman I hated.'

'And you loved it when I fucked her. You wanted her too, didn't you? Admit it: if I left you, you could be with a woman just as easily as a man.'

'Are you going to leave me?'

'No, I'm not. But you know what? If I did, you wouldn't see it coming. You just have to trust me. You'll be a lot happier when you learn you can't control your whole life the way you want to.'

'Only you can do that, right?'

'I don't control your life, Maya. Or if I do, you let me. If you hate it so much, why do you let it happen?'

'I don't know.'

'Well, you won't know unless we do more. See if you like it, and if you don't, we'll stop. But before you try it, you can't know.'

'First tell me what it is.'

'That'd spoil it. You'll see. It won't involve anyone else, just you and me. I'll show you.'

After our conversation, I am nervous for a while, wondering what is next. But then I begin to relax a little.

For our first anniversary, Ilan gives me beautiful stationery with both of our initials on it, and I give him a rare edition of *Lolita*. We have a romantic dinner together, and he tells me he does want to have children with me someday – just not now.

I am ebullient; I had feared he might never want to have children now, because it would break our bargain. It makes me think the bargain, too, might end someday – maybe even someday soon.

Ilan has stopped looking over the responses to the ads, and is no longer scheduling meetings with other women. I begin to suspect he may not do anything new after all. Instead, we will simply be able to move on to a quieter phase of our life.

During this time, I get a lot of writing done. My ability to write seems to ebb and flow in me like an instinct or drive. Sometimes I write quickly, as if in a fever. Other times, the words come to me more slowly and steadily, like drops from a dripping tap.

On the days when the writing flows quickly enough to allay my anxiety, and Ilan is affectionate, I am almost happy. This time, he is the one helping me. When he reads my writing and edits it, his small corrections of my wording seem to echo the small corrections of my body that he makes during sex, as he shifts me, above or beneath him, to increase his pleasure.

As the months pass, Ilan continues to be sweet to me – almost as sweet as I remember him being in college. He begins to bring me flowers every day – the ones I like best, Gerber daisies and white roses. I have been so long without them, I realize. And he rents another summerhouse – far from the one where I caught him cheating – so that we can have more peace and quiet to write.

I begin to believe he is falling in love with me anew – and I begin to fall for him too, to feel just as I did when I was nineteen, standing in front of the library, and he startled me, and it all began.

When we make love during this interim time, I fantasize that we are still in the innocent years before we married, before our bargain was made. I imagine us in a classroom, after Ilan has forced its lock; I feel us there against the hard table, breathing. I feel his weight on me and I love how it presses me down.

Or I imagine that we are in the field near my mother and stepfather's house that we once visited, long ago. The leaves crackle and crunch below us. Rolling on them, we reduce them to their netted, ghostly spines; shards of the leaves' skin shift lower in the pile below us. Among the leaves, on the dry grass, I am wet and ardent; I am – or I once was – alive.

I dream leaves into my hair. I dream him above me. I dream us, always, alone. I dream that love exists, that it can continue.

My next interview, which happens in September, is for me the strangest of all. Again an actor asks me to his house. Again he is alone there, without publicist or assistant or photographer. But this time the reason is very different.

The actor takes his shirt off casually, with his back turned toward me, as soon as I enter, and the sight is overwhelming: I have to close my mouth so as not to whimper with desire. I can't think, and for a moment, I can't hear. He speaks to me, but it is as if all the sound has been drawn from the room somehow.

'What did you say?' I breathe.

He taunts me: 'They say you know people better than they know themselves. But I know myself very well. So I wondered what you could possibly learn from me.' He has a slight accent, Australian perhaps. I remember that he grew up there, but moved away when he was a child.

I pause, dry-mouthed. He is the first man I have wanted since Ilan, and I am unaccustomed to it. He watches me, observant, uninvolved. He is more Ilan than Ilan is, I realize – lighter and less regretful, equally passionate and more headstrong. He is Ilan in a dream, in another life, in a fairy tale in which his soul is sweeter and his face more angular, as if he had been formed to be a tempter none could resist. Though I have met, in my interviews, many beautiful men and women, there have been none as beautiful as this.

'Come sit on the couch with me,' he invites. 'Try your best. See what you can get from me.'

I do. And strangely, though he has insisted he will never reveal himself, he does.

When I write up the interview later, I explain how much he misses his estranged daughter – although he mentions her name only once, I still can sense the longing, the crack by which his heart is riven, his loneliness.

'How is your daughter?' I ask.

'Oh, Stacey,' he laughs. 'She's growing up, doing fine.'

A single mention, the way his voice varies just slightly when he says her name, gives him away.

I observe his bored game-playing, sense his indifference to the arousal he invokes in women – in me. All he has in his life is sexuality, as easily as sunlight it comes to him. It means little.

He is getting older, in his forties now; his daughter is only five. She has a life in another country that goes on without him, and as each day passes, it is a lost day to him, whatever vanities he may have filled it with. The only woman he wants, he cannot have brought to him. And so he has brought me here, to carry a message to her, whether he is aware of it or not.

There are no framed pictures of her on his mantels, no photo albums on his shelves. But I know about hiding photographs – and so I look for the places where the photographs should rest, and do not. I can almost see them in their drawers: the girl in her swing, the girl on his shoulders.

When the interview appears, a month later, the actor calls me up crying. He tells me his ex-wife has finally brought his daughter to visit, after she read the article.

Now, he says, he sees I was right: his daughter was the reason he called me up, invited me over, though he did not know it himself, at the time. And, he says, he would like to see me again.

I do not go to see him. But I do allow myself a small infidelity: I keep his cell phone number in case I need to call it someday. And someday, much later, I do call.

The day after the telephone call, with the actor still on my mind – the way his shoulder muscles had tensed in the day's failing light; the sound of his

109

crying, the way it broke up his words on the phone –
I am distracted, not entirely present.

'Did anything unusual happen?' Ilan asks. 'You
seem different. You've seemed different ever since
that interview.'

'Nothing happened,' I reply.

'I think it did.'

'You're crazy, then. What do you think happened?'

'I don't know – something. The actor made a pass
at you, didn't he?'

'Right, this famous actor made a pass at his
married interviewer.'

'Dismiss me all you want,' he says. 'I know something happened. Look at you. You're glowing – it's
disgusting.'

And despite myself, I blush.

I have broken the spell – or his jealousy has. Afterward, Ilan begins to carp at me again – asking me to
revise one of his articles over and over, telling me it
is not good enough yet, pushing me even though he
knows I have a drop-dead date of my own, when I
must turn in my interview, coming up very soon.

I almost think he is purposely trying to trip me
up at times – to force me to weaken my articles
suicidally, so that even his father will not run them;
to tempt me to squander my small success. But it
doesn't work: I'll stay up all night if I have to, work
every waking hour if I must, until the moment I

finally email the piece to the office for my editor to review.

I begin to long for that moment, as if the email were not only a communication with my editor, but also a strange communication to some other self of mine, the self in me that is a writer at the core, saying, 'All is well, we are alive, I have found you, you are hearing from me again.'

The next interview is done on schedule, despite Ilan's sabotage, and I gain the next cover, and I know then with certainty that I can live if I leave.

Enough calls are coming in, enough offers to sustain me. In my own small world, I am solidly famous: my name is a brand, standing in for the secrets I have been told, the secrets I am now supposed to have an almost magical ability to elicit.

The college dropout, the least-loved child, the sulky and radically introverted girl – all these are myself, but there is another, shadow self, too, that I might yet become: an influential journalist, someone with power. Someone who can say, like Ilan's father, that she hires college graduates even though she never became one.

There is a possible transformation that is inside me, yet to occur: another person I could be, when I thought I could be only this one. And I would make the transformation, I would claim this other self, if it were not for this love – the love that became my life, that replaced it. I still love Ilan, even though I know I should not; he is still at the center of me.

Soon the first snowfalls of the winter arrive. We stay inside more and more frequently, in the comfort of the loft, with the heat on high. As we spend long days inside, Ilan's bad mood only worsens.

At the corners of each of the apartment's huge windows, ice crystals collect and build. I fantasize that someday the crystals will converge on the centers of the panes, and our view will disappear entirely – the small spots of remaining light blinking out all at once: a row of television screens darkening in slow motion into pinpoints, or perhaps the surfaces of a series of ponds, with their softish ice freezing solid above me.

Across the street, on the white vista of the playground, with their wary young mothers on the sidelines, children play in snowsuits. I look at them with a jealous hopelessness, as if they were unapproachably far away, playing instead in space suits on the moon.

Finally, the day comes when Ilan chooses to start his next experiment, to begin to teach me what he'd like me to learn.

I go to bed first, while he is still working at his desk. I'm curled up beneath a thin white sheet when he finally comes to me.

First he blindfolds me from behind. Then he lays cold metal on the side of my neck, tilts it so that it touches me. In the overheated loft, it is a relief against my skin, like the curved side of a cold glass of water touching it. It lies against me like a heavy necklace, clammy. I shiver. I feel its contours against my skin, its lines, and I realize it is – it must be – a gun.

'I'm your murderer,' he says. 'Lie still.'

Ilan knows about the actor, I can tell – knows I was drawn to someone else. And he knows, too, that I forgot about him for hours, that it was as if he did not exist, and he cannot bear it. He senses the threat, and this is the threat with which he has chosen to meet it.

He puts the gun in my mouth, lays it between my breasts. Then he eases it inside me. He moves it too slowly to hurt me, waiting endlessly for me to open around it.

He says, 'I am your rapist.'

'You're my husband,' I tell him, but he doesn't answer.

He pushes the gun inside me and makes me come – come so hard that I cry and cry. And then he comes without my even touching him, merely from the thrill of using it on me, simply from that.

The next day, I feel appalled at myself, dirtied by the game. Wanting to be alone, I leave the house long before Ilan awakens, and take the subway up-town to the Museum of Natural History.

The butterfly exhibit is long gone, I know, but I remember it clearly. I begin to fantasize about thousands of butterflies landing on me and together lifting me – the infinitesimal flutter of each of their wings amounting to a great soft upward rush of wind, as they bear me up. But then I know they would not come to me that way, not after all that has happened.

Instead I would find them clotting my mouth, my throat, my ears, my eyes. The collection of their small, petal-like softnesses would mean not grace, but suffocation. And it is a place deep within the ground to which they would bring me. Still, is it not a beautiful way to die?

I stand in line for a ticket, tall among a group of children on a school trip – boys who are, perhaps, young versions of Ilan; girls who are our lost daughters. Once inside the museum, I crouch to read the explications of dinosaur bones that are written for children and posted on knee-high plastic plates mounted on pivots.

I last about an hour at the museum – craning at the biggest skeletons, thinking about how all we get of the dinosaurs are their bones, and only frag-ments of those. What of their lives: the secret lives, unchronicled, lost forever?

I like the way that simply looking at the bones

makes me feel empty – as if in looking I become blank. Nothing can be expected from me here. It is reassuring. It is only I who have expectations, of what I will see and learn, and they are very modest. A small diversion is enough, anything to take me outside of my mind a little, outside of this sadness.

I do not ask much. And what I ask I receive: I am empty here; I am no one. That is exactly what I want to be now – the white screen, the face without features.

By the end of my time at the museum, though I have not consciously thought about it, I have my answer: I am not going to leave Ilan. Not now. I might someday be able to leave, but for now I will not.

Ilan makes me come with the gun every night for a time. I never see the gun, black or silver; I never ask to see it. I am always blindfolded; it is just a cold touch to me. He uses it until he becomes inured to it, until finally even that thrill has worn off.

After that there are other nights, there is a razor blade. Ilan has a steady hand with it. He watches me first, cutting, and then he puts his hand over mine to follow my hand, to learn my touch – just as he learned years ago to touch me the way I touched myself so I could come. I remember his larger body on mine, then; his larger hand on mine, then and now. Always the encompassing flesh, powerful and comforting. I like that he is larger. I want him to show me how.

I know all about those girls who cut themselves, the so-called delicate cutters and the red script the blade draws on their skin. I know how they skirt the veins that lie underneath like gray-blue rivers with tributaries that fade to nothing.

About a year ago, I interviewed a young actress and model who had once been such a girl, and who now had been told by her agent that it was a good idea, careerwise, to discuss it. And so she showed me her scars.

She had cut them below her bikini line so she could still model. I still remember her white, perfect skin and the way, when she pushed her jeans down for me, the scars of the blade's scratches showed beneath. I remember how I blushed, looking at them, and how, looking at me, she blushed too, suddenly embarrassed.

I know about those girls, but this was a little more than that. A little deeper than a scratch, with a little more pressure, bringing a trace of blood from the skin. And a little harsher than would quite be delicate, a little harder than the press a girl might exert in her pink bedroom, alone among her teddy bears. I do not scratch, but write in blood: the paper my own skin; the ending, perhaps, my own death.

Ilan warns me it is dangerous – we should avoid the veins, the ones near my wrists, he cautions, cut a little to the side of them, and he is careful that way. But still, the feel of his cut is harsh.

Harsh enough, indeed, that my skin remembers it. I had – I have – scars, narrow lines that cut across each other, as if the tips of tree branches had come to life and scrabbled at me like thin fingers. Marks that seem to suggest that someone, or something, once tried to kill me, but ineffectually so.

I know that something worse is coming, that it is coming soon, but I can only wonder what it may be. To avoid my anxiety, I begin to sleep a great deal. Ilan begins to be kind to me again, at least intermittently, and I take comfort in that, too, but mostly I sleep.

I wake up early or stay up late only to catch a plane to an interview, or to meet a deadline. Otherwise, I sleep, whatever time of day it may be. Ilan catches me napping at two in the afternoon and finds it hard to awaken me even then.

It's funny, when I was a child I was afraid of going to sleep, because I thought someday I would never awaken. If my father could disappear from my mother's house, I thought, perhaps I could too – spirited away one night, leaving just as my father left, without a bag packed or a good-bye.

It had been a time of disappearances. To prevent my own, I used to read with a flashlight next to the warm cat sleeping beside me – staying up as late as possible, until I fell asleep without anticipating it, without having to fear it in advance. Now it is being awake that I fear more.

My anxiety does not last very long, for soon I have my answer, I learn what can be worse. One night, Ilan tells me to wait for him – to wait in the shower so he can surprise me. Then he leaves the loft.

I turn on the shower and run it cold, so that it keeps me alert. I know Ilan will come to me, and I know what he will do will be terrible, but still I am not afraid.

I am waiting for the moment he alone can give me now – that moment of intense pain when it is as if I do not exist, that simple oblivion; the moment I know is inevitable and that I almost enjoy, so closely do I now identify it with myself. When I wonder why I stay, it is to that moment I return: the moment of immolation and purity, of intense sadness and perfect loss.

From the shower, I hear the door of the loft open. My back is turned as a hand reaches over my mouth. Water falls over me like a benediction. It takes a terrifying second for me to be sure it is Ilan, and not some other man he has chosen. But when I feel his touch again, I know.

His left hand stays over my mouth, while his right moves across my stomach to hold me still, then slides downward so he can put a few fingers inside me – so eager, in this first moment, to begin.

I bite the hand on my mouth. For realism, I draw blood. Ilan swears. Then he bends backward to raise my feet from the shower's floor, to carry me in front of him. Soapy, I slip through his hands a little and he almost loses my body, almost drops me, but he regains his hold.

As he pulls me from the shower, the point of my elbow hits the door's edge and resonates with pain. The glass door rattles, but does not shatter. His bitten hand bleeds on the tiled floor.

I fight, just as I am supposed to fight. I bite the hand across my mouth once again – although in some way, it feeds me. I am wild. I am, for a few moments, entirely unlike myself. I find that I like being able to fight until I am overtaken. It is like being able to scream in a car with the windows closed – your impulse muffled even as it is expressed.

In the bedroom it takes all of Ilan's strength to hold me down, and that is what I like the most, my inability to move. If my body can be stilled, perhaps then my thoughts, too, can be silenced. I hope he can put me back into the place of concentration I crave – the dream platform, elemental and white.

He ties my hands apart, not together. He uses neckties, not his silken cords. From such details I can almost believe he is really the stranger he pretends to be.

He likes blindfolding me; he doesn't want me to watch him this time. I like it too; it clears my mind. I realize the many ways I can recognize him, after all; the ways I know he is not a stranger: the way he thrusts inside me; the slight, characteristic smell of his skin.

With my vision darkened, I feel minutiae: the slight residue of the soap I had not yet quite washed off, as it dries into tiny flakes, the final drops of the coating of water that covered me as they evaporate. Then I feel nothing, and that is the best of all.

But then the pain becomes so intense, it returns me to the world. Small clamps he places on my nipples hurt sharply. I cry out, as he has wanted me to, but he does not answer, nor does he free me.

The line between the game and reality begins to blur: my cry, I realize, is real; I want him to release me. But it is impossible, I see that: I am full-service for him now, everything he's ever wanted. I am no longer a woman, but a fantasy of one; for now, I am no longer his wife, and he is right: he is no longer my husband.

I realize how fully I am demeaned, and I observe it all with as much detachment as an anthropologist might. Yet even in my remoteness, I begin to fear he will go further, and if he does, I'll be helpless against him. My life is slipping out of my control so quickly that it frightens even me; I have invited chaos in, but now I am afraid.

I feel Ilan straining not to get out of control, straining against the violence in him. I understand that once again I am close to extreme pain, even close to dying. And I know that I fear these consequences less than, by rights, I should. Who will save me, if not myself?

In the end, though, he does stop; he does leave. Alone, I walk naked to the shower from which I was hauled. I step into it gingerly and feel the water – I run it hot now, so it almost scalds – spreading through my half-dried hair. I close my eyes to the water.

For once, the image that comes before my mind is not of Ilan. It is an image of the actor, his back toward me, raising his shirt above his head – so casually yet with an impact he must know, must recognize, an impact as comfortable to him as skin. The image glows in my mind as my body aches, and it is to that image that I escape as the hot water trickles like blood through my sopping hair.

'One more woman.' Ilan comes to me and proposes it the next morning. 'One more time. And then it'll all be over.'

'It's over now. It's already gone too far.' I can't tell if he takes me seriously, if he knows how far in jeopardy our marriage is. As much as I love him, I have started to be able to imagine a different life.

'Give me this last night,' he pleads. 'Then we'll live like normal people. You want a child, don't you? A little girl?'

'You know I do.' I think of the actor's little girl, the visceral bond. Perhaps such a bond could save me. I would like to cry for someone beside myself, someday, as he did.

'You can have her,' Ilan assures me. 'We can have lives like other people's. You know, a happy family. We can be what other people think we are. I only want one more night, one more woman. I promise that will be it.'

'I don't believe you.'

'If I break my promise, you can leave me. I won't stop you.'

'You can't stop me anyway.'

'Yes I can,' he tells me confidently. I know he's right. I am lost without him, lost within myself. As much as I want to leave, I am still not ready.

'Go ahead,' I tell him. 'You're going to do it anyway.'

'It'll be the last time,' he repeats.

This time – the last time, or so Ilan claims – I am not blindfolded but gagged. He places the black gag over my mouth, ties it tight. For a few seconds, in panic, I breathe quickly through my nose, to confirm I can still breathe at all. But then I adjust, and relax my breathing.

Once my panic has passed, Ilan undresses me meticulously, folding each piece of clothing as he takes it off. Then he ties me up on the bed, with the silk cords he likes to use.

When he is finished, he ushers another woman into the bedroom. I have never seen her before. I don't know when he chose her; I only know that he did so without my permission.

Ilan undresses her in exactly the same way he undressed me: in the same order, with the same care. He folds her clothes in a single pile, next to mine.

Then she gets on her hands and knees above me, naked as I am naked. He takes out a razor blade and puts it between her teeth. She closes her mouth on it obediently, calmly. They've discussed this before; she shows no hint of surprise, her face serene as a Madonna's.

The blade she holds in her teeth, she now presses to my throat. Her hair is dark. Close up, I see it is dark brown – not red. There is no red in it at all. And she weighs significantly more than 130 pounds, I can tell. Her breasts are heavy and full, and her round hips curve above mine.

Lying below this stranger, with my hair spread out on the sheet below me, I can feel the merest touch of the blade on my neck, the slightest exertion of pressure. So far it is painless. Still, I begin to feel fear. Sweat seeps into my hair.

I think of what Ilan said, about being careful not to cut my wrists too hard – how even a small push on the blade could, in a second, cut a vein. I think of the large veins near my throat, so easy to find, to sever. I imagine blood running down the side of my neck, like a pearl-bottomed drop of paint.

The woman's eyes are solemn and sad. The blade shines in her mouth. But she does not cut me with it; she just holds it there against my neck, still with only the slightest pressure. I can't move, or I myself will inflict the cut. For minutes we are frozen there.

Then, as the woman holds the blade against my neck, Ilan starts to finger her, softly at first, then harder and harder. I can't see his two fingers holding her clitoris in their thin vise – but I can imagine them exactly.

I know the way his fingers slip around slightly, skewing off their motion as she becomes wet. I know how much it frustrates him. I know he is touching her now in just the way he likes to touch me, when he wants to make me come quickly: the fastest, the most effective way he knows. The two fingers, the fast rubbing, the helpless response – I know them well. But as always what I thought was mine, only mine, is not mine at all.

She lifts her head slightly, loses contact with my throat. 'Keep the blade down,' he cautions her. 'Keep it down, or I'll stop.'

She nods. He fingers her harder. He's getting to her, I can tell. I imagine she'd pant with arousal if she could – but of course she cannot, for she still must hold the blade. As Ilan moves his fingers harder and faster, the blade scratches my throat. I can tell that the woman doesn't intend to cut me, but in her pleasure, she squirms into it.

'Keep it down,' he says to her again, in a low, serious voice. 'Keep it touching her throat.'

The sting of the cut begins to spread outward from the line she draws on my neck. It's still just a trace, I can feel it is only superficial, but the pain is soft and warm and sharp, like a poison honey.

I watch Ilan get the distant look of concentration he always gets when he focuses on increasing his fingers' speed. And I feel her press the blade into my neck just a degree harder – because Ilan wants her to, and because right now she'll do anything he wants, as long as he does not stop touching her. I know how compelling he can be; how with touch, he convinces.

Suddenly the woman draws back a little, increasing the space between the blade and my throat. I anticipate that she'll lunge for my neck, or perhaps simply place the blade carefully, to make a deliberate cut. Pressing the blade down once, forcefully, might be enough – and it could happen so fast that Ilan could not stop her, even if he wanted to.

I watch her, waiting. But instead she carefully sits back, removes the razor blade from her mouth, and places it on the nightstand.

Visibly annoyed, Ilan puts the fingers with which he has touched her in his mouth; opening his lips, he skates the fingertips over the ridge of his bottom teeth, and looking at her, he licks them. She shudders with arousal.

'It's not over yet,' he tells her. He lifts the razor blade, its silver shine darkened with my blood, and offers it to her. 'Come back and finish what you started.'

'No, that's enough. You can hurt her, but I'm not going to help you. Do you ever let her speak?'

'I let her speak all the time, and even when she doesn't speak, I still listen.' He pauses. 'Now get out. If you can't keep your promise, I'd like you to leave.'

She dresses quickly and departs – angry, contemptuous, relieved.

We are alone. At the end we are always alone. This is supposed to be the end – the very end, it occurs to me. But it feels unfinished – the promise, whatever it was, unkept.

Ilan unties me slowly. The cords have marked my skin; red lines remain on my wrists and ankles. I have such fair skin that everything marks me.

126

I go into our bathroom to clean and bandage the cut on my neck. The sting of the Mercurochrome echoes the original sting of the cut's infliction. I place a white gauze pad over the cut and affix it there with adhesive tape. Then I put on the white shirt I was wearing earlier. I think of taking the gag off, but I do not.

I leave the shirt open as I look in the mirror. Though the cut on my throat is masked by its bandage now, the light scars on my arms from Ilan's previous cutting – or, rather, from my own cutting, with his hand over mine – are still visible. My unbuttoned cuffs fall back to reveal them, their white traces on my fair skin like lines in wax.

The delicate scars strike me as practice, practice for something that has yet to occur: the imprecise pencil sketches that precede the completed painting – with its thick, precise, final application of paint.

Who am I, I think as I look in the mirror, and when did this start?

Ilan walks into the bathroom to stand behind me. As soon as I see his face in the mirror, he says, 'It's over. It's all over.'

He reaches around me to button up my shirt, fasten my cuffs and remove the gag. Then he turns me around and holds me to him, as if I had been hurt by someone else entirely, and having saved me from that terrible man, he is comforting me now.

'It was the last time,' he says. 'I promise.'

'I am glad,' I say dubiously.

'You don't believe me?'

'Why should I? I could have died there. She was the one who decided I wouldn't, not you.'

'Well, that's not quite true. We can talk about that. I think you have the wrong impression. Do you want to have dinner, Maya?' he asks me nervously.

How long has it been since I have seen him nervous, uneasy? Even with the actor he was only jealous, angry – not vulnerable this way. He finally knows he could lose me – I think he does, at least.

'We could go someplace nice,' he offers a second later.

'Sure,' I say. 'We haven't gone anyplace nice for a while.'

'This was the last time,' he repeats.

I only shrug. 'Where do you want to go to dinner?' I ask him.

We choose a small, dimly lit Japanese restaurant a few blocks from the loft. At dinner Ilan feeds me, slipping small, fat dumplings into my mouth with slim metal chopsticks that he handles deftly. We barely speak throughout the meal.

We share a wooden platter of sashimi. In my mouth, each piece feels for a moment like a second tongue.

For dessert, I order green tea ice cream and like

that it is bitter. I feel it melt across my tongue, sticky and viscous and strong.

When we've finished, we linger at our table and talk of what we're writing, not of what he has just done. He tries to sound happy about my success – suggesting more actors to interview, other secrets they might hold.

I can barely listen, though. I know this is the moment when I should leave him. I should carefully explain the reasons – reasons that should, anyway, be all too evident by now – and then I should present my decision.

I am close, but I can't quite do it. The feeling is powerful, and yet hard to explain. I had thought, when we married, that our marriage would be a house, twisted and crooked but solid, that I could live in all my life. Now I hesitate, waiting on its threshold, unable to close the door.

Back at the loft, Ilan grabs my shoulder and says urgently, 'Why won't you talk to me, Maya? I know you're thinking things you won't tell me.'

'This whole time, were you ever scared I'd leave you?' I ask him. 'You just go further and further. Did you ever think you'd lose me?'

'I knew you wouldn't leave,' he says, and my heart sinks: is he right? 'You would never be able to be with anyone else,' he tells me confidently. 'Neither could I. For us, it's for life. You know that, don't you?'

'I can leave.'

'No, I don't think you can. But we can end this. Things can go back to normal.'

I only snort and say to him nastily, 'I doubt it.'

I don't know why I can't help him with this; it's almost as if some part of me wants it never to stop.

Ilan leads me into the bedroom. He reaches under our bed and takes out a metal box and places it on the bedspread. Then he opens it, and hands me a package covered in soft cloth.

I open it gingerly, for I feel how heavy it is, and there it is – the gun: small and silver and seemingly delicate, but heavy in my hand, its cold weight both familiar and strange.

'It's only an object,' he reassures me. 'Nothing magic, nothing we can't overcome. It's going to be yours now, not mine. We can keep it for protection. We'll drive upstate some weekend and I'll teach you how to shoot.'

He shows me how to load it, how to work the safety. Then, while it is still loaded, he hands it to me. I point it at him. Then I take the safety off, the way he showed me. As my life with him has taught me, anything is possible.

'You're kidding, right?' But he has an edge to his voice.

'It's only an object,' I tell him. 'Don't be scared.'

He puts his hand on the barrel and brings it

slowly down. I don't resist him. He takes the gun from me, replaces it in the box, and slips it deep underneath the bed again.

'I'm willing to do whatever's necessary for us to stay together,' he says quietly. 'I just need you to tell me what that is.'

'The gun isn't the only issue,' I tell him. 'It's everything. We're past the point where we could solve it. The woman you brought here, what did you ask her to do? Was she really going to kill me?'

As I finally voice the question, I feel almost as if I am awakening from a dream, unable to believe that what we've done could have been real.

'No,' he says slowly. 'She was just going to go to the edge.'

'If she'd made a mistake, I would have died. You could have killed me. You might have loved me once, Ilan, but you don't love me now.'

'Of course I do. Since the day we met I've been obsessed with you, and you know that, Maya. I love you just the same as before, don't you see that? Maybe even more, because now I know what you're willing to do for me.'

'I love you too,' I tell him – and it is the truth, I know that as I say it. 'But I still don't think you can ever change.'

'I'll show you,' he promises.

*   *   *

After our conversation, Ilan and I begin to seem, at least from the outside, almost like a normal married couple – our life full of ease, devoid of outward sorrow.

I interview another actor, find out another confidence – it is easy, since now the subjects are strangely eager to divulge them to me. Believing I will find their secrets out anyway, the interview subjects at least want to be able to try to charm me into writing a favorable piece.

Ilan begins work on an article too – about the long-standing claims of an affair between the mayor and his aide. The rumors have gained some new credibility now that the aide has been fired and the mayor has a new girlfriend. Ironically, there are some rumors that they played S&M games together, which Ilan will doubtless repeat in the article as if, to him, they are shocking.

To prove a point to me, I think – to prove that he has changed – he is writing the piece by himself; he does not even ask me to look at it before he submits it. I do not see it until it is in print, and when I do, I tell him, truthfully, how good I think it is, and so does his father. For once, his father's compliment means something to him – means a great deal.

Ilan seems content in our new life. Yet one thing troubles me: he sometimes seems strangely preoccupied, distant. At movies, I look over and see him in rapture. If I whisper something, he does not hear. He is more alone in his thoughts than I have ever seen him, as if he is deciding something without me.

He sleeps unusually late – so when I rise, rather than rising with me, he only ducks his head down beneath the covers, into the warm space our bodies' heat has left. It reminds me of how I used to sleep to escape him, and I wonder if he too feels the need to escape something – perhaps our odd normality, or his uncharacteristic fidelity.

After a few weeks, we begin to have sex again, but only rarely, and in only the most ordinary way. We do so as if our bodies are fragile.

One night Ilan slides away from me, carefully reaches inside me, and adeptly, painlessly, he pries my diaphragm out.

'The child,' he says. 'It's time.'

'Okay,' I breathe at him.

For the first time since one foolish night in college, there is nothing protecting him from me, or me from him.

'I can feel your cervix,' he whispers.

'I can feel you in me,' I whisper back.

And with nothing between us, we couple. He moves on top of me. My arms hook under his shoulders; my breasts press against his chest. My legs hold him to me; my arches are fitted, once again, to his curved calves. As his narrow hips twist him farther inside me, he rises up on his strong arms and kisses me deeper too.

This is our marriage as I always wished it to be – I feel how it could have been all this time. Our sex that night feels very intimate, almost disturbingly so, and I realize how little emotion has gone into it for so long, how different being aroused is from being moved.

It makes me wonder if there is a lost happiness inside me from years ago, sealed off, immaculate, that could someday be born in a child. I wonder if Ilan and I could change after all, if a child could change us, change the deadly pattern we have followed like a plan or destiny.

I remember how I used to believe secretly, especially when we first married, that what would end my arrangement with Ilan would be my pregnancy. The writing room, I thought, would someday become a child's room, and the trysts would end. With our little daughter playing in the loft, Ilan could never bring the women home.

Over time, I had forgotten how much I wanted this child. But somewhere underneath, I still did. Now I feel the wanting again – starkly there, a pure force. Each time we have sex without contraception, and we do so many times in the weeks that follow, it seems to sharpen.

I even begin to dream of children – though they are never delivered naturally, only by cesarean. Always, I am cut open, and blood seeps out of the cut and is stanched. Always, the babies bloom like flowers from the tuliplike white shells that surround them as they are lifted from my sundered womb. The child – Ilan's child, dark-haired and pale, real and otherworldly – is lifted out in her white sac. A scalpel opens the sac, and I touch our daughter.

Again and again we try to conceive, as if conception would break the pattern, as if this tiny new life would give us new lives too.

Maybe it is that way, sometimes, for other people, but it is not that way for us. Twice, my period arrives exactly on the day it is scheduled to come. The only difference is that this time, I cry at the sight of the blood.

Ilan reassures me that it's only been a little over two months – I'll get pregnant soon – but I think he sees the blood as I do: as a bad portent. Rather than being graced with a child, it seems we will only have more of the blood that lately has been everywhere. It is as if blood is seeping out of the sides of our lives; as if our lives themselves are dying.

Nevertheless, we keep trying. Spring coaxes out all the mothers, or the nannies, in the neighborhood, with their babies in their jaunty strollers, and I see how tired yet happy they all look. For our second anniversary, Ilan gives me a machine with which we can listen to the baby's heartbeat when it arrives, and I give him a dwarf rabbit in a cage, telling him that the baby will like it too.

As I wait to see if my next period will come, I watch Ilan closely for signs of the transformation he has promised me. And he does act as if he's changing – he is romantic, caring, tender toward me all the time, in a way he rarely has been before.

It should make me feel hope, I know, but I feel an irrational dread instead. I fear that Ilan is not changing: he is merely holding off. However much he speaks about it, I still wonder whether he truly wants a baby, wonder how he is tolerating our current monogamy.

Secretly, I begin to believe that he may be imagining something he can do that will be so bad, I will have no choice but to leave him. But I wonder what could possibly be so bad as that, when everything that has come before has not been enough to convince me.

I fear what will come, and at the same time I want it to happen, so that at least everything will be over. I know I should leave – preempt this final blow – but I am too frozen to do so, and since Ilan has tried so hard to keep his promises, I don't know how I could explain my leaving. He has been perfect, the perfect husband.

Months of trying to conceive pass, until we are well into the fall, and I am feeling desperate for a child. I almost forget the feeling of suspicion and dread that haunted me, so absorbed am I in my worries about when I will be pregnant. Each time my period comes, I cry. I had not known just how much I wanted a child until I began to try to have one.

One day in October, in order to distract myself, I go into the office for a while. I chat with an editor for hours, and then finally sit down to work. But when I do, I realize I have forgotten an important disk, and I return to the loft in a taxi, shielding myself from the rain and wind. From outside, I can see that all the curtains have been drawn.

The first floor rolls by as the elevator quietly rises. As I cross our threshold, I hear a door banging in the wind and feel a draft of cold air. My first thought is that a window is open and I must shut it; a storm is beginning, and the draft will only increase.

'Ilan?' I call out, but he doesn't answer. I intuit and I fear, my heart quickening, that there is a woman here. I am home hours earlier than I said I would be. It is as if I am back at the summerhouse, about to look through the fan – about to see her.

I see it first out of the corner of my eye, and then, in dread, I turn to see it directly. On the white wall is a single, partial handprint in blood, smeared in its imprinting, like a child's print on curling construction paper to record the size of his hand.

Ilan is on the leather couch just below it. His dark eyes are closed. Blood covers his sliced wrists, running in trails down their sides. The cuts are deep, directly on the vein, the kind he told me would surely kill.

He must have put his wrists up to his face at some point, because there are streams of blood caked on his eyebrows and eyelashes, too, and blood has dried in his hair in odd, dark clumps. It stands up in places as if mussed from sleep.

On the floor, the printed swoosh of a Nike logo is the only relief from the blood footprints.

I kneel down and hold him, hold his wrists as if I can close them now. A great sob comes out of me. The bedroom door keeps banging senselessly in the wind.

'Fuck you. I did everything you wanted,' I say to him quietly, and I repeat his name until it is just syllables.

I lay my head in his lap and cry. I kiss his face though it is covered with blood. I lick his eyelids as we have done in sex. It was so sexy to feel the jumpy eye move, unquiet, underneath its lid. Now the eye is still.

When I draw back from him, I see that the blood on his face is interrupted. My tears have trickled down his cheeks as if they were his own. No tear streaks were there before, and I realize he must never have cried, not even when he began dying.

I curl up in his arms for a moment, my head on his chest, but I can't stay there. I crumple from the couch to the floor.

I lie on my back, as if I am floating. I look for tiny calmnesses: the feel of my soles flat on the floor; the coldness of the wood on them, that slight gradient. I jam my nails into my palms the way I do at the dentist – to evoke the little, distracting pain that makes the larger pain slightly better.

Sometime later, I call the police. I tell them, as if in a dream or a movie, that my husband is dead.

Before the police come, I take from Ilan the chain with the metal hand, the one his grandmother gave him to protect him, and put it around my neck. When I move, the hand swings back and forth, clicking against my sternum – an erratic metronome.

I think of how the silver hand has lain on his chest for so many years, beneath his sweaters and above his recalcitrant heart. I think of how it hung above other women when he was with them, and how in the same way it hung above me.

I wear it now, I feel it against me – the fingers of the small metal hand trailing on my skin as if on the surface of water.

*   *   *

As I wait for the police, I decide I can't bear to look at Ilan anymore. I stare instead at the Nike symbols in relief upon the floor.

When the police finally arrive, officious and dripping with rain, they cordon off with yellow tape the couch on which Ilan's body lies. Then they make me sit off to the side, in the untouched part of the apartment, which still looks just the same, like a showroom for life next to a showroom for death. I lean heavily against the back of my chair there, and watch them.

There are two officers, one a detective. Stepping over the tape line, he begins, with gloves on, to examine Ilan's cut wrists.

'A suicide,' he pronounces.

'I could have stopped it,' I say to myself quietly.

'Many people feel that way,' he tells me, over-hearing. 'Trust me, it's not true.'

Instead of answering him, I begin to cry – wildly, pathetically. I am without shame; I don't care if the police hear. Let them hear me, I think: they are strangers.

'You're in shock,' the detective informs me. 'We need to take you somewhere where you can rest. Who can we call to come pick you up?'

'No one.' I can think of people who would come, even my parents, but no one I want to see now – only people whose presence would make me feel more alone. I know Ilan's father has to be called, and it would be all right to have him here, but I would like to give him just a few more hours before the truth catches up with him, like an animal let loose to find him.

'We need to take you to the hospital if there's no one,' the detective tells me. 'We can't let you stay here, not in the state you're in. It's the law.'

'Fine,' I reply. 'Can I sleep there, at the hospital?'

'Sure you can.'

'Did you look for the note?' I ask.

'There doesn't appear to be one.'

'I'm certain he would have left one. He was a journalist, a writer.'

'Ma'am, I've been searching around here pretty thoroughly,' the second police officer interjects. 'If there'd been a note, I would've found it. That desk is locked though' – he points to the writing room – 'so I'm going to force it, okay?'

'No, don't do that,' I tell him. 'It's my desk, not his.' But I lie. The locked desk is his. I lie because I would like to open it up by myself, in my own time. And if there is a note there, I would like to read it alone.

'Sometimes people don't leave a note, you know,' the detective points out. 'They're not in a frame of mind to be able to.'

I nod, but then I say again, stubbornly, 'I know he would have left one.'

The detective is gentle, and I don't fight him. He

escorts me to the hospital and has me check myself into the psych ward, where I sign a paper that says I cannot leave until they let me.

At the hospital, I am put on suicide watch, in part because as soon as I change into my thin hospital gown, everyone can see the light scarring on my arms, the red line still healing on my neck – a second chain, like Ilan's, that I can never take off.

They give me sleeping pills but I don't sleep. All night, a nurse watches in the darkness from a chair near the end of my bed, a sentinel.

'I'm not going to kill myself,' I tell her. 'You don't have to stay.'

'It's my job,' she says. 'If you relax, you'll go right to sleep. You took enough medication to put a horse out.'

'My husband died.'

'I know,' she says. 'I'm sorry. My husband died too. Five years ago. A heart attack.'

'I'm sorry too.'

'Don't be,' she says. 'He used to hit me. My life is much better now.'

'Good,' I tell her. 'Good for you.'

'Go to sleep,' she repeats. 'In the morning you'll feel much better.'

Finally I do fall asleep, calm among the cheap, clean sheets, overborne by the chemicals, my mind shut by my heavy eyelids' weight.

142

That night, I dream that I detach from the world and rise away from it, as invisible threads break soundlessly. My dream is a dream of flying, and then of a sudden fall.

The next morning, another nurse wakes me, bringing me cereal that I eat but do not taste. She says people have arrived – my mother, Mr Resnick. But I tell her I don't want visitors, and she nods. I want some quiet time here, time to think, to be alone.

When she returns, to tell me that she has sent the visitors away and to give me the flowers they brought for me, she also gives me a tranquilizer.

Hazy and almost hallucinating on the strong drugs I have been given, I begin to think about what happened with Ilan. I remember being with him for the first time in my narrow college bed, so many years ago, when my heart raced for him – I think of how pure the love between us had been, and how we tainted it.

I admit to myself that all the experimentation with the women fascinated me as much as it hurt me – like an accident I was compelled to watch. It had the feeling of a car skidding on snow, the feeling of the inevitable.

It was such a natural progression, what happened between us – yet at the same time, a lethal one. And I let it happen. After a while, I did not question whether Ilan could be better. I believed resolutely that he could not. And I gave permission for something he did not really want, not in the end. Permission that was, perhaps, a dare. I was the girl who handed him the cigarette and said, Go ahead and burn me.

In the end, he had tried to change, and I think he was sincere in trying, but I did not believe in him, and he could not restrain himself. He would have killed me eventually: the cutting had started, it had continued, and I believed it would have completed itself somehow.

He died for me – died so I wouldn't have to. It is the only possible explanation for his suicide, at least for me.

I was not the only one he slept with, far from it, but I was the only he would have died for. Next to that, what could a touch, a kiss, the temporary enmeshing of the flesh mean? How could it ever matter? He offered me his blood, his breath, his regular pulse, when he could just as easily have taken mine.

That means he must have loved me – doesn't it? My silent question hangs in the air.

The psychiatrist who is assigned to me prescribes 20 milligrams of Prozac per day, and provides other medication to calm me until it begins to work. He offers me therapy as well, but I decline. Therapy cannot help me, I believe, since I will not feel comfortable enough to tell the truth even there. Ilan was the only one who knew the truth about us, and I do not want anyone else to learn it now.

At night I grind my teeth – awakening each morning with a trickle of blood on my pillow, and a tiny cut in my mouth. The blood again: it sickens me. I imagine that my mouth is lined with blood; that if I am ever again aroused, my arousal will transpire only blood.

Privately, I am still distraught, caught between escapist fantasies, the effects of strong drugs, and sheer grief. Around other people, however, I begin to be able to appear normal. My sense of shame returns, and I begin frequently to wear the single turtleneck I have brought, to cover up my scars, instead of the hospital gowns or the T-shirts I also brought.

Eventually I am able to conduct conversations without crying, and even able to convince the psychiatrist I am improving dramatically.

Finally, after about six weeks, I am released from the hospital, on the condition that I continue with the Prozac for a while. I promise that I will, and I do. As the weeks have passed, it has finally started to take effect. The drug cuts off the 'down' but I can still see it, as if I were walking on a pane of glass over a chasm.

Even my tears have Prozac in them now, it occurs to me. At first, taking the drug felt like a huge capitulation, a loss of self, but then I remembered it was not such a great self anyway, all told. Very masochistic, in fact. I would like a new one. If I could wish away my heart, I would.

When I get home to the loft, the day I am released, I am stunned by how different it looks. The first thing I think of is Ilan's handprint: I want to see it again and I can't. It's gone forever, overpainted. All the blood is gone from the leather couch, too, but that can't be. Is it a new couch?

The floor, too, is clean, bare of blood. The loft is spotless. I know Ilan's father must have had it cleaned, and I appreciate the gesture, but I am not yet ready to see it so pristine – as if Ilan had never died here. I miss the apartment the way it used to be, even the way it was when his body was here – as if it were an entirely separate place I can never visit now.

Opening the closet we shared, I discover that all of Ilan's clothes are gone. I find some of them hanging in a small closet near the back of the apartment. At least, I think, Mr Resnick was respectful enough not to dispose of them without asking me.

As I enter the closet, I close the door behind me. In the darkness I draw Ilan's clothes around me, like a child hiding. I can still smell, slightly, his cigarettes.

With tears in my eyes, I begin to search among his clothes for the keys to his desk. In the pocket of one of his jackets, I find instead the blindfold and silk cords. I can barely stand to touch them. Finally, in an inside pocket of another jacket, I find the keys. I slip out of the closet, keys in hand, and open Ilan's locked desk.

Its top drawer holds a long, thin envelope. The rest of the desk's contents are familiar: the metal box in which he kept the gun, his notes for stories, his drafts, his letters.

I open the envelope, trembling. But there is no suicide note. Instead, the envelope turns out to be full of childhood photographs of me – ones I know I didn't give Ilan. He must have stolen them from albums in my parents' houses. I realize with a pang that my parents never noticed, and that Ilan must have known they never would.

In one of the photos, I am painting at an easel, ten years old – unaware I am being photographed, inside that strict concentration I still retain. In another, I am eight years old, falling off my bicycle – caught in midair, when I am still absorbing the fact that I am falling, just in the moment before I begin to scream.

It is a strange, mistaken snapshot; I was supposed to be photographed proudly riding my new bike. I don't understand why my mother kept the photo, for her children always excel in everything they do. But I do understand why Ilan stole it: because I am so vulnerable there in the photo, about to be surprised by the hard contact of the pavement – vulnerable and open and astonished.

The photos – there are ten of them in all – make me cry because they teach me, one by one, in a flash, what it was that Ilan loved in me, in what respects and with what limits. They show me the qualities that drew him: the preternatural focus, the dreaminess, the vulnerability and the pride, the wounds concealed.

They show, more than anything, how before I met him, I was so profoundly apart. They show how far away I was when he found me, and over what a long distance I had to travel to come back, to come to him.

The photos show me the way he saw me. And now they are the way I see myself. I will show yourself to you, that was his promise; I know you better than you know yourself. Even dead, he does make good.

That first night at home, I let sleep take me very early in the evening. As I become drowsy, watching the light outside the windows fail and fade, it is as if I begin subtly to feel myself disappear.

As I shimmer out, I begin almost to see you, Ilan; the dark bruise-like circles under your eyes start to resolve. I cannot help it: my heart races with a mere glance, just as it did when you lived. Burning, I rise in sleep, like a body jerked upward by invisible strings – as if in a moment I will levitate. Pleasure runs through me like a tremor, like a seizure, like faith.

I cannot forgive myself for this, but equally I cannot resist it, and what harm can it do now? I dream of you, Ilan – dream as I have dreamed all my life of meeting you on a platform, empty and white, where we can tell each other the truth and the world is as I wanted it to be; where it is possible, as it never was in life, for me to love you without fearing you too.

I dream of you, Ilan, and in a moment, I will see you. The darkness around me, unaccountably, is opening into a pure white.

Ilan, I cannot wait until we can be alone.

The next morning, I am awake for a few moments before I remember Ilan is dead – the dream was so real, it so convinced me, that for a time, even waking, I am caught in it.

The memory comes to me like a strange and terrible sunrise, its light creeping inexorably across the floor toward me to illuminate my bed, my mind, my heart.

Ilan's father calls a few minutes after I have awakened.

'The hospital told me I couldn't visit, Maya,' he says. 'May I visit you now?'

'Please,' I say. 'I'd like you to.'

'If I'd known you were coming home, I would have been there to greet you. I just called the hospital and found out they'd released you yesterday. I'll be right over.'

I put on a turtleneck so Mr Resnick will not see the marks on my arms and throat. I realize I'll always have to cover my scars like this now – perhaps even with a choker and bracelets, in the summer. It reminds me of an eerie fairy tale I read in childhood, of a girl who always wears a ribbon around her neck until on her deathbed, her husband unscrolls it, only to find her neck has been cut in two.

When Mr Resnick arrives, he knocks hesitantly and politely waits for me to answer, though I know he has a key. He walks with a cane now, bent over as if Ilan's death has been literally a blow to him. If I even stretched my still-healthy body in front of him, it would feel like mutiny. I stoop and shrink in his presence.

He embraces me, but I find I don't like touching him. He still looks too much as Ilan would have looked, if he had aged. He is still as rangy and narrow-hipped and unconventionally handsome as Ilan – even as he is also curled in on himself and brittle.

I take his coat and the Russian hat he wears and hang them up. He sits down on the couch, painfully slowly.

'Are you all right?' he asks. 'You were in the hospital a long time.'

'I'm okay. I can make it, I think.'

'I'm glad.' He pauses. 'Did you see anything, Maya, in the days before?'

'I wish I had but I didn't.'

'Nothing?'

'Nothing.'

I start to cry, from guilt and from wanting to tell him the truth, yet not being able to – and perhaps because he too has started crying; I can see the tears beginning at the corners of his eyes.

'Mr Resnick,' I say, 'if I had seen anything – anything – I would have told you. Maybe he slept later. He might have been more distracted. Probably I should have known, but I didn't, I didn't see it.'

'It's not only you, Maya. I spoke to Ilan every day, saw him several times a week. I saw nothing. You know, he came by the day before it happened – to see his mother's room, he said. At the time it didn't strike me as unusual, he used to come there quite often when he was younger. Now I wish I'd asked him why. He must have been saying good-bye to her. Or saying he would join her. They were always so close, you know. I never could compete.'

I twist my wedding ring on my finger, suddenly

conscious of it. My impulse is to return it to Mr Resnick. It seems somehow that again it is his – or, more precisely, his wife's. But I do nothing, for fear of offending him.

'Do you know why he did it, Maya?' he asks me.

'I'm not sure, I think he was just depressed. I thought we had a good life. I was happy with him and I thought he was happy with me, but he must have been feeling a lot of pain I didn't understand.'

I don't even sound convincing to myself. Mr Resnick only nods.

'I was completely in love with Ilan,' I add, glad to be able to tell at least one truth. 'As much so as when we married. More so.'

'I know you were. That's what bothers me. He had love, he had what he wanted. I don't understand, I can't. To see his mother die from cancer, when she would have done anything to live even one more month, and then to do this.'

'I don't understand it either,' I tell him. But I don't think Mr Resnick believes me; he senses there is something I won't disclose, but he is too discreet to press me further.

He tells me that, as I assumed, he's the one who had the apartment cleaned, and I thank him. 'If you want, we'll get you a new one,' he says. 'You just say the word.'

'I want to stay here.'

'Yes, of course you do. But tonight, perhaps, you might want to stay uptown?'

'If it's not too much of an inconvenience, yes, I'd really like to. Last night was hard,' I tell him. He nods.

After the previous night's heartbreaking dream, I look forward to sleeping elsewhere. And I have an ulterior motive for going uptown: I want to see Ilan's mother's room, the last place he visited before he died.

During the taxi ride, Mr Resnick asks me again if I am okay, really okay – and even touches me, his hand over mine for reassurance.

When we arrive, he shows me to the living room and sits down across from me in an upholstered chair. A maid serves tea. I don't drink from my cup; I only hold it beneath my face, to feel the steam on my skin.

Again Mr Resnick presses me for answers; again I gently resist him. Finally I ask to see Ilan's mother's room, and he leads me there. Its marble floor is still bare. I think of Ilan as a child, sleeping beneath his mother's bed, his cheek pressed to the cold marble.

'May I sleep here?' I ask Mr Resnick.

He is startled. 'There's a very nice guest room down the hall.'

'But I'd like to stay here, if it's all right.'

He nods. 'Yes, it's all right.'

*   *   *

As soon as he leaves, I slip below the bed, to lie as Ilan lay, but it does not make me feel better, as I had hoped. The floor is the same cold marble, but the past is still the past; I am not haunted except insofar as I haunt myself. All is quiet here. And still I dream of a supernatural life, one that could transport me; I dream of somehow being able to see Ilan once again, one more time.

After a time I slide out from under the bed and rise up. Curious, I open all the dresser's drawers – wondering about the woman whose ring I wear, the woman whom Ilan loved so much and who left him.

She kept everything, I realize – from the dresses she wore in the flush of health, styles from the Sixties and Seventies, to the soft fleece sweater and sweatpants she must have worn in her last illness. And her husband has kept everything too.

From one of the dresser drawers, I select a plaid pair of pajamas. As I fasten them around my waist, I am unnerved by how well they fit, but then I remember that, as with her wedding dress, I have been tailored through surgery to fit them. Then I fold down the covers and climb into bed, but soon there is a knock at the door.

'Come in,' I say quietly.

Mr Resnick inches into the doorway, with a glass in his hand. I can see that he notices the pajamas, but all he says is, 'I'm sorry to disturb you. I thought you might want a glass of water.'

Late at night, I notice, his face relaxes, until he resembles a much younger man. I imagine for a second that he looks as you would someday have looked, Ilan, if you had lived.

In the moonlight, the glass of water shines. I drink it down like a cure.

'I'm so unhappy,' I confess. 'I want the pain to go away. I want a new life, where it doesn't hurt so much.'

'A new life, yes, of course you do. I thought that with Ilan's mother for a long time, years maybe. It's only human. But I was wrong, of course. There is only the one life. You already have it. There is no need for a new one.'

'I'm sorry. I didn't mean any disrespect.'

'Of course you didn't.' Mr Resnick reaches out to touch my arms, as they lie on the coverlet, and I feel lucky that the pajamas are long-sleeved; they cover my scars. He leaves his hands there for a long time, as a healer might – almost as if he knows the scars are there.

He tells me then that Ilan had a trust; the amount is in the millions, and it is mine now, I am entitled to it. It is still technically revocable, for complex tax reasons, he explains, but he will never revoke it; it is mine.

I am shocked. I had never paid much attention to

money after we'd married, because I had known there would always be money enough.

I realize the trust must have contained money meant for my children's – his grandchildren's – college educations, for their first homes, for *their* children. It is a trust for ghosts. Still, I thank him for it, and for once I keep myself from crying.

Mr Resnick talks in a hushed voice of finding me a psychiatrist, of my reconciling with my parents, of my writing again. I realize that he has more hope for me than I have for myself.

In the middle of the night I awaken, my mouth tasting of iron. I turn on the light. When I put my finger in my mouth, I draw it out stained with blood.

Frightened and dazed, I spit the blood into the glass of water Mr Resnick has left for me. The blood slowly unspurls into dark strands. As it loosens it also, and very slightly, trembles, like the netty leaf of an undersea flower. Drifting downward it comes undone, its dark red spreading out to color the rest of the water.

Staring at it, I am relieved to realize that it must be the teeth-grinding again, nothing more. I rise and go to rinse out the glass in the bathroom sink. Feeling inside my mouth for the cut, I find it, small and tender, the mark of a tooth's point on the inside of my cheek.

The cut; the cause. It is only a physical wound. Nothing to worry about, I reassure myself. But I am nervous. The blood was supposed to have stopped, but it is still here with me.

In the morning, Mr Resnick begins to question me about Ilan again, and I realize I must leave. As much as I might wish to, I cannot help him, because I can never tell him any part of the truth; he could not bear it.

I return to the loft, and that night I sleep on the leather couch where Ilan died, as if I can somehow be close to him that way. I almost expect to awaken covered in blood, but I do not.

At Ilan's service, three days later, my family escorts me like a group of bodyguards, flanking me as I sit. Though Jewish tradition is to bury the body quickly, the funeral has been held off, the body kept frozen, so that I could attend.

Ilan's father's speech is moving, yet as I did at my wedding, I feel lost. Ilan's colleagues speak as if they had truly known him, when I know they never came close. They praise the writing I submitted for him as if it were his own. They claim he had all sorts of virtues he never possessed, and they miss the one that was really his.

He loved deeply, obsessively: for me, that was his saving grace. He loved me more than life. Sick as it was, it was a powerful love, and for a long time it was the love I wanted, however dangerous it may have been.

After the speeches, many of the journalists come up to me to express condolences, chatting with me in low, confidential voices as if they know me well, and I realize they believe they do, because they have read about me, or read my interviews.

I am introduced, then, to one of the effects of my small, new fame – the false familiarity; the attempt at an unearned intimacy; the ugly, desperate wanting of the gifts they believe I can bestow.

Strangers accompany me on the walk to the grave, and strangers watch with me as Ilan's coffin is lowered into the ground. It is part of a double plot that lies next to another double plot, which contains Ilan's mother's grave. There is a grave next to hers, I realize, for Ilan's father – and a grave next to Ilan's for me. I imagine for a moment that on Ilan's tombstone, under his name, is mine. I think of how someday Ilan and I, and Mr Resnick and his wife, will all lie immobile here, like four dolls in our underground beds.

Strangers speak to me, and try to console me, and even provide me with the white rose I toss into the suffocating dirt, the dark opening that will be Ilan's new home.

It is so strange and terrible, and their familiar

words are almost disorienting: I do not care if they are 'sorry.' 'Sorry' is much too little to be, and I am not sorry, I am something else entirely. Destroyed, perhaps. Or grateful.

Ice crystals shine in the broken earth on the sides of the grave, and I try to concentrate on them, willing every other thought from my mind. I try to block out all the black-suited journalists somber at the graveside; to pretend that I am here alone, and that it is I alone who must fill, with a heavy shovel, the wide grave where the coffin waits to drown.

I wait at the grave for a long time, until only I and Mr Resnick and the gravediggers are left standing there. The gravediggers fill the grave with dirt, and then they leave, and still I wait, until Mr Resnick kindly leads me away.

For Ilan, I remain the quietest girl, the stillest waiter. I continue to wait, but I don't know, anymore, what I am waiting for.

The next day the *Times* runs a short, kind obituary that talks about Ilan's writing and says that he was 'survived by' me, his 'wife and colleague, the journalist Maya Sumner.' In fact, I do not 'survive' Ilan. Instead I begin to become a different person through his death, I can feel it happening.

Now who knows what the new person – born in a death, inside its black and sticky caul – will do? I am too tired to become someone else, but despite myself, change will come to me, I feel it. Ilan, who will I be without you?

After the funeral, Mr Resnick calls me frequently – to check on me, he says. And sometimes he'll stop by. But I am quiet at his approaches. Not rude, only quiet – like the child I once was. The girl was underfoot, she is gone; the adults resume their talking. The line between quietness and disappearing is a tenuous one. Gradually Mr Resnick's calls and visits fade away, becoming more and more infrequent.

For a while, my mother checks on me often too – because she feels she should, I am sure; because she knows that is what a mother does in such a situation. She coos with sympathy. She drags my stepfather into the city, convenes my half sisters and half brothers here too; makes recriminating calls to my father, demanding that he explain his absence. There are crowds and coffee cakes for days. I am lucky it is still winter; I can always wear turtlenecks and long sleeves so no one sees my scars.

But after a time I am alone again. My family shouldn't be faulted for leaving: I have always been a difficult child, an ungrateful child, and as they draw away from me, feeling my ingratitude, I draw away from them too, and toward Ilan – as I have done ever since he first took me out into that empty

Connecticut field. Even in death, I am still his, and his alone.

Somehow the days pass. Often I rent movies, but I watch them through a haze. In one, a flock of birds descends on a jungle gym, and only a moment later do I remember to find it threatening. All the birds have alighted and still I am slow to fear them: were I a character in Hitchcock's movie, I would doubtless die.

Yet despite my frozenness, I nevertheless keep writing my magazine pieces. I feel as if my byline's appearance is, at least, proof I am still alive.

I always file by email now, speaking to editors only on the phone. I want to put off, for as long as I can, returning to the magazine's offices. I fear it will be too hard – too hard, especially, to see the new interns at the desks where, only a few years ago, Ilan and I once faced each other and finished, late the same night, the first articles we wrote.

I do not want to see any of the people there whom I once knew or who, more accurately, were once my passing acquaintances; they will only pity me. And I am quite an object for pity now, for I look terrible, this death has aged me all at once.

Lately, I have skipped all the appointments I used to make to try to be pretty for Ilan, to be as pretty as the other women, I hoped: the manicures and pedicures, the body wraps and hair colorings. I have let my nails grow, my hair become unruly – as I imagine is happening to him in his dark grave. I have stopped caring about being pretty, since he is not alive for me to be pretty for.

I pull myself together only for my interviews – putting my hair up and hiding it beneath a cap, clipping and cleaning my newly stubby nails. The interviews, I know, are good for me. They force me to fly places, to speak to strangers, to become the woman with the laptop and sunglasses next to the hotel pool. They force me, even, to smile a hollow smile that feels borrowed from someone else, or some other time.

In front of the actors, I pretend sanity and am accepted as sane. They seem to notice nothing. Used to being the center of attention, and caught within their own anticipation that I will tease out their secrets, they seem barely to notice me, playing out their own dramas as I watch.

Knowing them, seeing them for what they are, becomes easier and easier the quieter I become, and so my interviews improve and deepen. Eventually I start to realize that my depression has actually benefited my interviews. And my reclusiveness, it seems, has equally increased my fame – enhancing the impression that I have secret access others do not, that I move in exalted circles.

Though I do not appear in public anywhere, the gossip columns have an answer for that: they simply make up places where rare spottings have occurred. I attend the Oscars, according to them; I have dinner with, become close friends with, several celebrities whom, in real life, I merely interview.

The interviews take up only discrete segments of my time: two days to conduct them, three or four days to write them up. The rest of the time, I write about you, Ilan – it is the only writing that truly occupies me now.

I complete the interviews hastily on my laptop, but to write about you I return to my desk in our writing room. With my back turned to your desk, I can imagine you working there too, just behind me.

Still taped above my desk are the photographs that accompanied my Siberia article – the one about the lovely actress who moved with her actor husband to the middle of nowhere, an absolute seclusion where no one could reach them. Now, though, the photographs have changed for me. The icy vistas and the couple's angular, modern house are the same, of course. But what used to seem austere and beautiful now seems to me only dull and blank.

On my neck the red scar fades to white – the traces of the collar I wore for you. On my sternum, still, your tiny hand hangs. On my wrists the white ghosts of your cuts remain. You still captivate me; my mind and heart are marked just as deeply.

As I write, I see my own bias but I do not bother to correct it. Passion is bias to some. I write emotionally, riskily.

Simply writing about you feels strange and dangerous now – the way our love did when you lived. Sometimes it feels almost as if my life were a piece of paper being folded dangerously smaller and smaller, a tight packet I can never leave, a story I am writing that entraps me.

As I write, I begin with your three expressions – the ones that I saw only in sex, that you forbade me to tell you about in Italy. At the time, I did not even silently describe them to myself. To do so would have seemed a betrayal. Now I permit myself to think, even to write, about the way you looked, the way you will always look to me in memory. It is your eyes I remember most clearly, with their dark underlying half-circles of gray-smudged, grainy skin.

Here is what I would have said to you then, if you could have borne it. My descriptions are simple, and not so shocking or embarrassing after all.

First, there was an expression of pleading. Second, there was one of pure want. Last, there was one that was brutal and acquisitive and foreign – one that I hated, that I loved, and that aroused me, all at the same time; that triggered in me a mixture of feelings that I now associate with you, as closely as I do the very image of your face.

These are my descriptions, but they do not satisfy me. In the end, I am consummately alone with these expressions. Had you been able to see them yourself, you would have revised them, for they were too naked, too open. Had I described them to you, you would never have shown them to me again. Now I cannot describe them fully even to myself – let alone to another person, let alone to you. But I can see your face before me as if you were alive.

I wish that while you lived, I'd had a secret camera – if only so that I could give these three expressions away to another person, if only to keep from keeping them inside me, where they reside. If only to be allowed to give this story, this life, away, instead of keeping it inside me where, again and again, it reopens the deep cut of your death.

Part 3

One day in early May, about eight months after Ilan's death, the buzzer sounds, interrupting my writing. I am working on a piece based on another interview with the gay star, who now claims he's actually bisexual, and I am annoyed to be interrupted.

I look down from the window to see who it is – a woman I don't recognize. I take the elevator down, and open the door to the street.

The woman has straight auburn hair and fair skin. The bright pink sweater she wears is a color I thought was forbidden to redheads, but it suits her.

I don't need a scale to weigh her, or a tape measure to know her height is precisely the same as my own. She is 5'9", 130 pounds – exactly. If she were to wear my clothes, they would fit her perfectly. She could impersonate me, seamlessly replace me in the world.

Uncertainty skitters in me: what is she doing here, now? She is from a past that can't exist anymore.

'Hi,' she says, and smiles. Her smile has pain flashing in it, pain and uncertainty. We resemble each other even in the incompleteness of our pleasure.

She glances down at the scrap of paper in her hand. A set of shiny bangles on her wrist shifts as she scrutinizes it. I can see that it bears an address, and in a moment I make out that it is ours. And that is Ilan's handwriting, I'm sure of it – as another little fishhook leaves another little scar.

'You're Maya.'

'Yes.' I open the door wider. She slips past me, into the building's foyer.

'I'm Olivia. Is Ilan here yet?'

'No. I'm not expecting him either.'

'I'm sorry,' she says, flustered. 'He asked me to come today, I'm sure it was today. Didn't he tell you? He said you'd be expecting me.'

'I might have forgotten.'

'Do you mind if I come upstairs? I'm curious to see the apartment. A triangle, isn't it? It sounds very cool.'

'Sure,' I agree. 'Come on in.'

The small elevator seems uncomfortably close as we ride up. I usher her into the loft.

There I ask her, in a tone I hope is casual, 'When did you meet Ilan?'

'Oh, nine or ten months ago. At a bar, I forget which one.'

He met with her shortly before he died, I realize. And he broke his own rules: the rule that I would meet the woman first; the rule that she could not know his name, or mine. But these are such small infractions now, interesting only as evidence. They don't touch on the real questions: why didn't he cancel? Did he intend for her to come here even after he had died?

'I thought it was weird the date was so far in the future,' she continues. 'But he said he'd be away for the time in between. Didn't he tell you I might be coming by?' she presses, uneasy.

'No. What did he say when you met?'

'Look, is something wrong? I could go.'

'He left me. Just after he met with you. I don't know why he didn't cancel this.'

'I'm so sorry. The way he talked about you, I would never have thought. He said I shouldn't make a mistake and think he didn't love you. He said he was crazy about you, and this would be a one-time thing. No one would get attached. He told me he was faithful to you except for this – that was exactly what he said, "faithful except for this." It appealed to me. I didn't want to break up anyone's marriage. I just wanted to . . . you know . . .' She pauses. 'Did you do this for him all the time?'

'Sometimes.'

'And he still left you.' She says it thoughtfully, with consternation.

'Do you think he might come back?' she asks. She gets me on that one. I blink back tears.

'No. I think he's gone forever.' For a few moments, we both fall silent. I am lost in thought, fighting to contain my tears.

'It's amazing how much we look alike,' Olivia ventures.

'All the women looked like me. But you look like me the most.'

'Do you think it meant anything? Besides the standard twin fantasy?'

'I don't know, but it can't have been good. I would rather not think about it.'

'Then we don't have to talk about it,' she assures me.

She sits down on the black leather couch, sits just where Ilan's body once lay. The handprint would be right above her head. It *is* right above her head, under the paint. It's just that you cannot see it there.

'Were you attracted to Ilan?' I ask.

'Wasn't everyone? He's the type of guy who's not objectively that attractive, but . . .'

I laugh, startling myself, and then cover my mouth, embarrassed. The first laugh since his death, it had to happen someday.

'Yeah, that's exactly the type of guy he was. Once he said to me that he wanted, just once, to hear a woman say that objectively he was very attractive, but personally she didn't find him sexy. I told him that wasn't ever going to happen.'

'It hardly mattered to me how he looked,' she tells me earnestly. 'I was in this for you. He showed me photographs. I thought you were beautiful, very sexy.'

'But you also wanted him. You can admit it. Everyone wanted him.'

'Not me. In fact, I made a deal with him that he couldn't ever touch me, he could only watch me with you. I don't know what you guys did with the other women, but I wanted you, not him. And I'm still sitting here wanting you now. If he left you, that's his mistake.'

There is an awkward silence, but she does not let it last long. 'Can I kiss you?' she asks me.

I hesitate as Ilan's pattern plays out in my head. We are supposed to go to the writing room, where he will join us, and that is impossible now – so shouldn't I stop this, say no to her?

Instead I nod, and in a second the rules are broken. Suddenly I am being kissed on the couch, and kissed with some passion that has little to do with fantasy. There is an absent way you can be kissed by someone who is thinking of what to do with you next – Ilan's way with me sometimes. And then there is this other way, the way she is kissing me now, with a sweet, heedless immediacy.

I am not strong enough to resist her, not in this

state of mind. I am not even certain – since, in a way, he has sent her to me – that I should.

'He was crazy to leave you,' she says, touching my face. 'You know that, don't you?'

'I try to tell myself that.' If I am not careful, this double entendre – his death as a mere departure – is going to bring me to tears again, and then my tears will be a sort of lie too.

And partly for that reason, so as not to lie anymore, and partly because I feel so alone – because I have been, for so many months, so alone – I take my blouse off and slip her soft pink sweater off, and we move into the writing room, and it begins the way it always does but slower, and far more tenderly. She joins a little gallery of women in my head but at the same time she is different, she is herself.

It is hallucinatory sex, uninhibited because it is out of sheer and pure despair. There is no conscience inside me anymore to feel shame, to hesitate. I have willfully cast off the self that would have felt these things. Like a sleepwalker I move purposefully but in a trance.

She holds me from behind, with her hands first on my breasts, then pressing on the insides of my thighs. The shiny bangles on her wrist scratch me slightly as she presses harder. Then she is opening my labia, to touch them. And it is as if I can hear Ilan saying 'so soft,' 'so wet,' close to my ear – doing little more than breathing the words, the way he would when he would touch me there.

I shiver again. All I do is shiver now, it seems. The posture is so odd, with her touching me as she holds me from behind. It is as if my body is still being presented, for show, to Ilan. As if she were offering my breasts to him, as they have so often been offered to him by other women; as he has so often taken them with his hands and tongue. I think, You are the ghost now, Ilan. This is the life that goes on without you.

I have so many memories of being here with him and they are so strong, but it's funny, in my strongest memory I cannot even see him, I only know he is here. In this memory, I am on the bed with one of the women, and he is in the closet, though she doesn't know it yet. He has yet to open the door to reveal himself. In this memory, he is only watching, as I imagine he watches me now.

If he were in the room – if he *is* in the room somehow, a ghost, a silent watcher – he would see my body shiver with pleasure and my face, with pleasure, convulse.

He is here as Olivia and I face each other; as she brings her nipples to her own lips and licks them so I can watch her; as afterward, she brings my nipples to her lips and licks them, too.

He is here, I know it, as she moves delicately toward me, holding her breasts forward, to touch her nipples to mine, like circuits connecting; as I shudder with arousal at her slightest touch.

He is here, later, as surfaces are breached, the way he likes them to be: so soft, so wet, so inevitable the penetration. So sweet the second seduction – to give in to her, now, as I once did to him, and yet not to feel unfaithful, because I believe he wanted this, he planned it.

She takes me to orgasm and beyond it, she takes me there several times, and for the first time in so long, the way I come is the willed, concerted way I learned from Ilan long ago, in college and after – not the forced way, achy and compelled, in some respect unpleasant and in some respect alluring, that he later taught me and that is, to me at least, an entirely different pleasure.

This pleasure, the only one I have allowed myself since he died, I accept entirely. I lose myself in it, and for moments I almost forget that he is gone.

'Do you miss him?' Olivia asks me afterward, lying next to me in bed.

'Yes, I do.'

'You'd still take him back?'

'I don't have the option.'

'What if he came back? Then would you?'

'I guess I would.' I know I would. 'But he's not going to, I'm sure of it.'

'Why did you let him sleep with other women?'

'Well, that was the bargain. He told me before we got married it would be this way.'

'You're not answering my question, Maya. *Why* did you agree?'

'It was the choice I had, so I chose it. Lots of women make choices like that, they just don't admit it. They know their husbands cheat and they ignore it.'

'Lots of women *don't* make those choices too. You could have had a different kind of relationship.'

'Not with him I couldn't.'

'With someone else then.'

'There was no one else.' But I lie: there was the actor, I think there could have been the actor.

'You deserved someone who wasn't abusive to you,' she says carefully.

'Ilan wasn't abusive,' I retort. 'I chose what I did. I knew what I did.'

'But you didn't want to do it.'

'Not entirely,' I admit. 'Not all the time.'

'And he made you do it. And now he can't. So there's a good side to his leaving, isn't there?' She strokes my shoulder gently.

'Yes,' I agree – defeated, unwilling to fight her logic. But the truth, though I don't tell it to her, is that I want him. I want him back. I liked it, and I couldn't leave it, and I would have died of it, if he had not.

*   *   *

I let Olivia stay in my bed that first night. I realize there is no reason anymore for our rule, Ilan's and mine, that the woman has to leave. The woman can stay. It is not personal to let her stay, to have her sleep beside me. A dog or cat would have been welcome that night, any breathing thing in the bed beside me, its breath a charm of life.

As I go to sleep, I think of the longer, more truthful explanation I might have given Olivia when she asked why I stayed with Ilan. I would have explained, I think, that the most jaded people often start out as the most vulnerable; there must be a world of soft expectation for it to seal over so hard. That the cold persona that is developed for someone else's benefit can steal inward, until you mistake it for yourself.

And more than this, that there is something alluring in giving yourself up to love, or even simply to another person; in giving up the control that is tiresomely exercised, insisted upon, in every other part of life.

All of that, I would have told her, and then the kick of that helpless coming. Helpless, hopeless, exquisite. The self in yourself brought back to you in a flash of feeling, of closed-eye seeing. Is it really so hard to understand, so easy to dismiss – my love for Ilan, my inability to forget him?

*   *   *

In sleep, Olivia and I curl up together. In the morning, as I awaken, the back of her hand is on my mouth, so much softer and smaller than a man's would be. It feels so small and fragile that I lift it and move it aside, rather than brushing it away or simply turning my head away from her.

While we are still in bed, I tell Olivia that Ilan died. I tell her I lied to her, explaining that I didn't want to tell a stranger the truth. She is not even fazed. Instead she accepts the news calmly.

'Maybe it's fate,' she says, 'that I still came to you.'

'It's not fate,' I scoff. But I don't tell her to leave. Instead we go to brunch, and for the first time in my life, I tell someone a little of how it really was with Ilan. On a wooden table, next to our bagels and fruit, our cappuccino, I lay my arms out for her and she touches, gingerly, my scars.

When we return to the loft, I give myself up to the tears I have so far restrained. Olivia holds me and lets me sob in her arms, until I make myself sick from crying. Afterward she tells me to lie down, brings me a cold cloth, and holds it to my forehead.

Olivia stays with me again that night. The next morning, she asks if I'd like to spend the day with her, and I say yes.

'I have a surprise for you,' she tells me, and asks if I will walk to SoHo with her.

'Of course,' I tell her. Today I have nothing else to do – I am between interviews.

She leads me to the Prada store, on the corner of Prince and Broadway. It is huge and strange, with a circular interior glass elevator, a central sloping panel of light wood, and huge naked, headless male and female mannequins.

She leads me to a dressing room on the first floor, and asks me to stand there in front of the mirror. It takes a few seconds for me to understand, but then I see it: the mirror is on a time delay. I realize then that it is not really a mirror, exactly, but a screen, and I look for the camera that must be recording us – for the image we see is not the image of us in the present, but in the very recent past, perhaps a few seconds, even a minute, ago. I find it, a black machine staring down at us from a high corner of the dressing room with its single eye.

It is then that Olivia begins to undress me, and I her: I would not have been able to endure the exposure if she had not joined me in it – if she had not led me to it.

Olivia licks my face, my breasts, kisses the back of my neck. Before the mirror, and its camera, she undoes me.

I am naked not just for her, but for the camera, exposing my breasts to it on purpose, giving it seductive glances, just so she can see the images a

few seconds later. I worry for a moment that someone else might be watching us too, but then Ilan's
words again come back to me: Let them watch us,
they are strangers.

Our sex is urgent, slick, passionate and intimate,
exhibitionistic and private at the same time. There
are knocks at the dressing-room door, but we ignore
them.

Soon we fall into a cycle in which we kiss and
touch each other, and then stop and watch the last
moments of what we have just done – both as an act
of voyeurism, and to delay our pleasure in order to
make it all the more acute when it arrives.

In the images, we too seem at moments like
mannequins, so similar to each other do we appear.
We seem to have been cast from the same mold,
almost to share the same skin and eyes, as identical
twins would.

There are only small differences between us:
Olivia has light stretch marks on her breasts and
thighs; they are just discernible. And I, of course,
have all of my scratched scars. But these contrasts
are tiny, and barely show up in the mirror. Often a
second passes before one of the red-haired women
in the tape turns her head and shows her face to the
camera, so that we can tell ourselves apart.

Olivia puts her hand in my mouth and lets me
bite down on it, so that no one will hear my cry, and
then I do the same for her.

We dress silently, slip out of the dressing room, and walk like any other shoppers through the store – still not knowing if somewhere a camera recorded it all, or if somewhere, our sex is being played for someone on a screen.

Afterward, we walk out into SoHo disoriented, intoxicated. Olivia suggests we go to a movie, and I realize I have not seen one in a theater since Ilan died. In all that time, I have only rented videos, mostly for the company they provided – rented perhaps a hundred by now, in the months that have passed, the number a measure of how much I have stayed inside, how many days I have been alone.

Traveling to the theater – the Angelika, only a few blocks away – we are caught in the middle of a rainstorm, which is violent but tepid. The rain soaks my long skirt until it is heavy with water, douses Olivia's suede jacket, darkening it until it changes color. We take refuge in the foyer of the theater, and then we wait in line.

We sit in the calm of the warm movie theater, the audience silent in the darkness, the screen lurid with color. My skirt drips as we watch, clinging to me. I touch Olivia's hand. I feel so sexual with the wet skirt on my thighs, I want her so much.

The movie is good, excellent in fact, but I am agitated.

'Let's go,' I whisper to her, and she nods, I can tell she feels the same. What happened before the time-delayed mirror happened so recently, but still it was not enough.

Heads turn to watch us as we exit – two redheads who might be sisters but who touch each other as if they were lovers, walking urgently up the aisle, leaving a movie everyone knows is good. Since it is too dark for me to be recognized, the stares only amuse me as we run their gauntlet.

Outside it is still raining, and we slip into a cab and dash into the loft, waiting impatiently as the elevator rises, following our own momentum into bed.

Our wet clothes drip heavily on chairs. The wind drives the rain against the closed, curtained windows. In the dark, Olivia's red hair appears almost black.

I begin by caressing the deep scoops of space under her arms, with their gray shadows even after she shaves. I touch the lush, fleshy breasts that slip slightly to the side in crescents as she lies there supine. And I pass my fingers over the two creases that slice her lovely neck horizontally, like quick, healed cuts in the skin – cuts inflicted on her only by time, by its gentler and slower blade.

Then I am down between her legs, my hands under her hips to tilt them, my fingers pressing deeply into the muscles in her ass – hard muscles that she flexes when she is aroused. I want her almost as much as I once wanted him. Yet for now at least, I love her less. For once, I am the one who takes advantage.

Olivia moves around so she can lick me too. We tongue each other delicately, reveling in each small flinch. Each of us copies what the other is doing and I imagine, when this happens, that our bodies really are exactly the same.

I shift my hips away from Olivia and slide toward the foot of the bed, until she is no longer touching me; I touch her and that is all. I want her to concentrate solely on her own pleasure; I want her to watch my red hair spread out over the bed below her as I touch her and lick her between her legs.

It makes me happy to watch her lose herself this way. I will not reveal myself today, but she will reveal herself to me, I will insist on it.

I watch her face tip back as she forgets I am looking at her. I watch her stop caring how long it is taking for her to come. I watch, and it is erotic for me to watch, as she becomes consummately selfish for a time: there is only this one thing in the world and she will have it.

I see in her an inexorable wanting, strong and desperate. I watch her mouth as it opens and stays open, as it goes slack. I listen to her small murmurs of pleasure. I watch the way she is unprotected, unashamed.

Beneath my tongue and my fingers, I feel her hips rise and fall. I move my hands onto her hipbones, framing the cup of her white belly. She rises and falls with increased urgency. Despite herself she begins to spread her legs wider and wider, until she reaches a degree of spread that is highly in-delicate – a physical posture that connotes to me every time in life that I have wanted too much, and what the consequences of that have been.

She spreads for me; the extent of her wanting overcomes me; I am wet, myself. Whatever she wants, I'll give to her. I bend my neck, I press harder, I am farther down inside her with my tongue – imagining it rough as a kitten's, imagining that I create friction as I lick her soft labia, tease her clitoris out from beneath its small, cowl-like hood. I am insistent, I concentrate, I can wait.

I wonder to myself – as she rises to me, as her pleasure takes her, as I put the flats of my hands on the flats of her thighs and press on them hard, as I show her she can spread even farther than she believes she can – as I do this, I wonder if I will love her. And I wonder if she can make everything I once was, and all I once wanted, seem to me only surpassingly sad and strange.

*　　　*　　　*

185

The next evening, Olivia invites me to go dancing at a club she likes on the Lower East Side, and I say I will. I calculate that the club is probably too obscure for any journalist to be likely to see me there with her, and even if there is a report of my being there with another woman, I know I can always deny it, and Mr Resnick will never believe it. When he last saw me, I was hardly in any condition even to leave the house.

Again Olivia meets me at the loft – wearing a bright red dress that provides a shocking contrast with her red hair. Since we met we have barely been apart.

As we walk to the club, I feel a soaring, there are the lights of faraway hotels, and I know it is wrong, in the wake of Ilan's death, that I am so happy – that in this time, of all times, I have caught sight of such a clear pleasure in myself, like pure water.

I try to allay my guilt by thinking: He sent her to me. She is the one he wanted me to be with. In a way, she is the note he left for me – I believe she is, at least. In everything she says and does, I believe he somehow speaks to me.

The club is hard to find on its shadowy block. Once inside, in the darkness, with the music a roar in my ears, I am incautious – letting Olivia touch me as much as she wants, dancing with her in a way that would convey to any careful watcher that we sleep together.

I watch another woman flirt with her, try to dance with her. For once, I do not enjoy my jealousy in any respect. Instead I instantly dislike the woman – who is short-haired, small-boned, bubbly, birdlike – and I want her to go away. It makes me wonder whether Olivia is actually changing me after all; whether this is the kind of love most people know, whether I could have it too.

Olivia turns away from the woman and begins to dance with me again. She whispers to me, 'Ecstasy,' and then she leans over to kiss me.

I take the pill from Olivia's tongue without a second thought – maybe because the petite, flirty woman is watching us jealously. I've never tried drugs before; for all our sexual experimentation, Ilan and I never experimented that way. I think it excited him that I – and the other women – would do what he asked with the aid of nothing more than a little champagne; he loved that drugging us was unnecessary.

The Ecstasy takes a while to fade in, but when it does I feel the love it inspires, and I try to forget that the feeling is fake. I accept it just as I accepted the kiss.

When Olivia sees I am starting to be affected, she slips a pill into her own mouth and smiles at me. Soon I see the shine in her eyes from the drug's euphoria, and I wonder if there is a shine in mine to match it. Wherever she takes me, I want to go.

*   *   *

We stay out all night at the club and watch the dawn from its roof. Then I take the subway home with Olivia, both of us in dark sunglasses. The sunglasses are mostly for privacy; I fear running into a journalist on his morning commute.

We are not quite hungover yet; instead we are still slightly drunk. We giggle together, sitting in our low-cut dresses with the suited morning travelers in the tarnished subway car, its floor tracked with footprints. It is not a life I am used to, this life, but I find that it suits me in a way.

At the next stop, some of the people near us in the car filter out, and when they do, they reveal a single, dirty footprint, with a Nike swoosh in its center, outlined on the floor.

Suddenly I envision the prints on our white floor, in Ilan's blood; I see him walking, weaving, falling, see his eyes closing. I hear him slump into the couch, watch him put his bleeding wrists up to his face.

I prop myself up on the metal arm of the row of seats so that I don't faint. I try to think of other things, to collect myself before Olivia notices my distress, but it's too late.

'Are you okay?' she asks me. 'Let's get some breakfast. The night is still young.'

'The night is over,' I point out, still reeling, trying to recover. 'But it was great. I had a great time.'

188

I try to sound happy, but I am shaken by the vision, and I'm sure she can hear it in my voice.

'You liked the X?' she presses.

'I loved it,' I tell her.

'I can introduce you to more,' she whispers, leaning closer. 'Whatever you want – you just tell me.'

'You don't have to do that.' Since Ilan and I never used drugs together, they still make me nervous, just as they did when I was a teenager. She looks dejected; I think she saw drugs as a new gift she could give me, a new surprise.

'The Ecstasy was great, though,' I add, to console her.

The rest of our ride back home is quiet. Another wave of nausea hits me, but I do not give in to it, I only lean more heavily against the cool metal and sink down farther in the plastic recess of my seat. I realize I have become one of the people I used to stare at on the subway, when I used to go to work.

By the time we go to sleep, an hour or so later, I have a headache from drinking, and from the drug – which has a terrible 'down,' I learn – and Olivia says she feels ill too.

We each drink water and take aspirin, put on icepacks. Then we lie next to each other in bed, with only our fingertips touching as we drift to sleep. In the dissipation of the pain from the headache, there is a kind of pleasure. And I find there is a calmness in my going to sleep beside Olivia that I never felt with Ilan. I am not afraid of what the next day will bring; instead, I am expectant, curious, almost happy to meet it.

These small pleasures, are they what constitutes a life? It might be as simple as this, I fantasize – the trick to happiness that I could never find, that I thought I did not believe in.

Soon Olivia is staying over every night. In the daytime, she spends part of her time in Brooklyn, at her apartment or studio – she's a photographer, it turns out – but I never visit her there. She was the one who came to me, and it stays that way.

Eventually I give her a set of keys – Ilan's keys – and finally, after she beseeches me to do so, I invite her to move in. She accepts instantly, and packs up and moves the next day, giving up her own apartment even though it means breaking her lease. I am disturbed at how much she throws away, how thoroughly she purges herself of her own furniture and belongings so they will not crowd mine, but I say nothing.

I take her into our house, mine and Ilan's, so quickly, so easily. And slowly I begin to give her access to all the places I used to let him in.

With Ilan, I became a certain type of woman, and I continue to be such a woman, I find, even after he dies. I am still easily overtaken, perhaps easily taken advantage of. Olivia's insinuation into my life is like another soft penetration, with a mixture of pleasure and a question of what I have permitted, what I have invited; like fingers offered to me to lick, the very gesture an assurance that I want what is offered.

It is so easy to say that I do want it, to take the fingers into my mouth when they are held out to me, to feel their whorls against the slight texture of my soft tongue. I do not question Olivia's entry into my life; I give myself up to it.

Occasionally I still think of the actor, but as time passes, I gradually forget him more and more; after all, I met him only once. And I feel very grateful to Olivia now, even though I know I do not yet quite love her. Without her, I know I would be wondering why to live. Instead, I am confident enough that my latest prescription bottle of Prozac sits in the medicine cabinet unused.

It turns out Olivia is a joy to live with. She is never in a bad mood, and she is always bringing home beautiful fabrics that she'll make into translucent curtains, or fabulous spices she has found in Chinatown. I tell her not to cook so often – I never do, and it makes me feel guilty – but she says she enjoys it.

Sometimes it is a little eerie, the attention she pays to me; at times her precision, her perfectionism remind me of Ilan arranging our wedding, making sure every detail was right. But then I remember that in a sense he was offering me the wedding as a bribe or a compensation, while what she does seems to be done purely out of love: she asks nothing from me except that occasionally I sit for a series of photographs.

She often uses a timer, photographs us both together, and doctors the photographs to mix our images, in ways that are fascinating to me; my face will merge into hers, or her hair into mine, which is slightly curlier.

She tells me she got the idea in the Prada store – that as much as she had wanted to be there with me, she had also, at the same time, wanted to be behind the camera watching the twinning, the strange echo of one body in another.

As I get to know Olivia better, I begin to learn the details of her life, everything from the mundane – her red hair is dyed, she's naturally a blonde – to the significant: she grew up in North Carolina, was a runaway, never finished high school. For years she drifted in and out of foster homes, halfway houses.

'It must have been terrible,' I console her.

'People survive worse. The important thing is that I'm here with you now. You suffer to get somewhere, that's what I learned. You do it for something – that's why it's worth it,' she assures me. I feel that beneath her confidence, she is reassuring herself as well.

It was photography that helped her attain a normal life, Olivia tells me. That, and her grandparents, who began to take an interest in her after she left home, and who still call often, paranoid, to warn her about the dangers of New York City.

'Without them,' she says, 'I don't know what I would have done. Do you have anyone in your life like that?'

'Ilan was like that.'

'No he wasn't,' she snaps. 'What did he ever do for you?' It's the first time she's ever spoken to me sharply.

'He helped me leave my parents.'

'You ask so little, Maya. You deserve so much more.'

As I learn more about Olivia's life, she begins to learn more about mine – the tired stories of my unpleasant parents and their happy remarriages; of my half sister's teenage pregnancy, and the strange way it made me begin to long for a child of my own.

I tell her little of the years with you, Ilan; she does not want to know. She knows about the women, of course, and she knows you cut me – I've shown her the scars – but she does not know about the gun, or about the last games we played just before you died, those games that were so serious to me. These last things, I don't have the heart to tell her, and I don't think she can bear to hear.

Most of our discussions about you are very simple. We fall into a little pattern, Olivia and I. She tries to convince me I did not really invite or deserve or want all that you did to me. I try, in return, to believe her. But within myself, I am torn.

For her, of course, everything that happened was your fault. The pathology was yours, never mine. Now that you have died, our lives will disentangle, and everything bad will stay in your grave with you; I will be free of it.

It was not my fault. Olivia has said it to me many times, and now I repeat it to myself: It was you, not me. It was you, not me: I chant it silently. It's you, don't you see, Ilan? It's you and it was never me at all.

Soon another interview leads to another cover story and another secret unveiled: the actress has long been addicted to painkillers despite public denials. She confides in me that knowing I would learn her secret anyway, she has decided to tell her own story, her own way.

It is odd how actors – even stars who have long been in the public eye, and are expert at handling the media – now attribute to me an almost magical power to ferret out their secrets, know them intimately. I didn't even know my own husband, I want to protest – not well enough to save his life, anyway. He had his own secrets, and I did not learn them. He still remains in part a mystery to me.

I visit the actress in rehab to conduct the interview. She is there for the first time, finally able to stop worrying that a visit will disclose her addiction, since she is now ready to talk about it herself.

Her face is peaceful but her hands shake – they shake with the need that she has not yet satisfied, that perhaps she will never satisfy. I know the story well, and so I write it well – as if it were my own.

For several months, my life with Olivia is quiet, romantic, untroubled. But beneath the quiet surface, a small conflict grows: even as she begins to use me repeatedly as the subject of her photography, I am obstinate in refusing to return the favor.

When I am not working on my interviews, I write more and more about Ilan – and never about Olivia. His is the body I never tire of imagining; his, the face whose angles echo for me now in strangers' faces on the street, as if it lived behind them.

While I take her body into my hands, I will not take it into my mind, I do not become obsessed with it. And she can tell.

One day I notice my journals are slightly askew – piled differently from the way I left them.

'You went through my things, didn't you?' I demand.

'No, I didn't.'

'It's obvious you did – look at them. You had no right.'

'Fine, I skimmed a page or two – that was more than enough.' She pauses. 'I want you to get rid of the journals. Will you do that for me? It's sick for you to obsess over Ilan like this.'

'But it's my writing, it's the way I'm working through it.'

She doesn't believe me, and she persists. Finally, to quiet her, I agree to get rid of the journals – to burn them, as she wants me to.

The next day, I pretend to rummage through the desk for my journals, annoyed that Olivia, who is in the next room, isn't watching. I find them easily – I always knew exactly where they were, in fact – but there is a distraction: I again come across the envelope of childhood photographs Ilan left for me, and cannot resist looking at them.

I slip the photos out of the envelope, and onto the desktop. They seem eerie to me now – especially the one that freezes the moment when I am caught falling off my bicycle. I used to think it showed vulnerability, openness; I believed that was why he chose it. Now it seems to show only how I can't stop time, can't stop the oncoming blood and hurt. I can't stop it, but my eyes nevertheless are bright; there is excitement in me, falling.

'What a strange photo,' Olivia comments. Absorbed in scrutinizing the photos, I am startled. Peering over my shoulder, she reaches over me to fan them out so she can see them.

'I'm impressed you recognized me,' I say quietly, my heart beating fast, as if I have been caught being unfaithful. 'I didn't look much like myself yet at that age.'

'I'd seen the photo before – Ilan showed it to me.'

'What? What are you talking about? I thought you only met him once. He showed you my photos?'

'I told you that when we first met.'

'I thought you meant photos of me the way I am now.'

'No, childhood photos. These.'

'All of them?'

'Yeah, all of them.'

'Why?'

'How should I know?'

'There must be a reason. He left them behind for me when he died.'

'Of course he did. It's just another way for him to control you. I'm sure he meant for you to wonder forever. He set these puzzles for you to solve, Maya. He left his death as some kind of macabre puzzle for you on purpose. This is the man who didn't leave a suicide note, remember?'

'Yes, I remember.' But, I think, *you* may be the note he left.

'Just forget about him, that's what he deserves.'

'You're right,' I tell her. 'Of course you're right.'

That evening, I offer Olivia a bag of ashes. Inside it, buried in the gray dust, are the charred, twisted spiral rings of seven notebooks, each spiral like the mangled spine of some metal creature.

Olivia is delighted, but she does not know the truth: I burned seven notebooks, but they were new, and blank. I bought them to burn them. The real ones – the ones in which I wrote of Ilan – I only locked away in his desk, as if I were saving my own heart in a drawer for the day when I would need it.

Taking the bag from me, Olivia smiles, and I feel a pang of guilt. Though I expect her to throw the ashes away, instead she disappears into our bedroom to stash them somewhere, as if they were a memento, remains to be kept in an urn. As if, Ilan, they were the last of you.

I believed that would be the end of her jealousy, but it is not. One night, soon afterward, I am sitting next to Olivia and she reaches out for the chain.

It unnerves me. I saw so many women reach for that tiny silver hand when it was around Ilan's neck, not mine.

'I really like your chain,' she says. 'What's it supposed to be?'

198

'It's Ilan's, from his grandmother. It's supposed to be the hand of God. To protect him.'

'Can I wear it for a while? I'd like the protection.' She lifts it over my head; it is off in a moment; and she places it around her own neck.

'No, I'm sorry, you can't. Could you give it back, please?'

But she makes no move to lift it from her neck. Instead she only looks at me levelly.

'Come on, give it back,' I repeat.

'Okay, okay.' She is laughing, but it is such a snorty little laugh, it reminds me of crying. She's hurt, I can tell.

Another moment passes. Finally she hands back the necklace – the small hand icon a charm in her palm, as it was in mine that first day with Ilan. The hand is the same, but I am a grown-up now – my loss.

The next morning I awaken to the feeling of a single finger trailing slowly along the arch of my foot. I start: 'Olivia!'

'I love your arches,' she says.

'Please don't do that. I'm jittery enough here. You scared the hell out of me.'

'Sor-ry,' she virtually sings at me. She's wearing my chain – Ilan's chain. I touch my neck instinctively, out of disbelief; she must have taken it as I slept. Quickly I segue my touch into a small rub, to try to mask its meaning. But she's noticed.

'I want the chain for a while,' she says. 'Please?'

'It's Ilan's.'

'I only want it for a day or two. I'm seeing a gallery owner today. I need a little lucky charm.'

'Okay, but I'm going to miss it all day.'

'I'm going to miss you all day,' she says. 'I'll call you later, okay? And I'll take you to dinner if I get the show.'

'Sure,' I say reluctantly. 'We can do that.'

When Olivia calls me later, she announces, jubilantly, that she got the show. Later, we meet at an expensive restaurant she has chosen.

'The necklace worked,' Olivia comments as she reviews the menu.

'Can I have the chain back now?' I ask her. I can't restrain myself, even though I know I'm being rude.

'Not now,' she tells me. 'Let me tell you about the meeting. I have all these ideas for how to arrange the work, it's a very interesting gallery, and it's divided in two, so I can play on the doubling, the similarity between the images of you and of me.'

I listen as carefully as I can, but find it hard not to be distracted by the sight of the chain. By the end of the meal, she still has not returned it, and I know I cannot ask for it again, not now. I can only hope she will return it soon, before I have to ask.

*   *   *

That night, Olivia goes to sleep before I do, and I watch her sleep – her mouth open, her face child-like, her eyes mere half circles. The hand on Ilan's chain is now hidden beneath the neck of the white T-shirt she wears; I can only see its links disappear at its collar.

I am tempted to lift the chain off her neck – as she must have done to me the previous night – but I stop myself.

It is only a chain, I remind myself, only an object. She wants it only because she is jealous, insecure, because she loves me and is vulnerable. And she is right to be jealous, right to worry; it is not mere paranoia. She believes I'm still in love with him, and she is right: I am.

I think to myself, If her only fault is that she wants me too much, that she wants all of me, how much of a fault is that? Some people would say I should be glad of it.

Olivia's show goes up about a month later, and it is well received. She has agreed not to use any of the sexual pictures of us together – I am afraid Mr Resnick will somehow see or hear of them – but even so, I am still nervous to attend the opening.

When I arrive, though, I find that I should not have worried: she has protected me. None of the images trouble me at all, except insofar as they are disturbing in themselves; none unduly reveals me. And Olivia adeptly conceals our relationship – joking to a reporter that she must be a true narcissist, since she has chosen a model who looks just like her.

She refers to me as her model throughout the opening, and for the first time in my life, I begin to feel truly beautiful. Though I know I don't look perfect, it matters that she thinks I do – that she believes my face, my body, are lovely and interesting enough to photograph. I was never complimented when Ilan sought doubles of me – I felt it must underline my inadequacy somehow, or his need to perfect me. But when she doubles me in her photos, I somehow feel greater: more powerful, more whole.

When we return home after the opening, I write for a while. Olivia says she is going to take a nap in our bedroom, and leaves me alone in the writing room.

I should be focused on Olivia, thinking about her show, about how caring she was toward me there, but it is Ilan who remains on my mind. I lose myself in writing about him.

When I finally look up at the clock, I am surprised to see how much time has passed. It was that way when I was in bed with Ilan too, I remember – as if our encounters occurred outside of time.

*   *   *

Hours later I enter the bedroom to join Olivia, expecting her to be asleep. Instead I find her sitting up on the bed, holding my wedding dress, in its plastic covering, on her lap.

'I found it in the back of your closet,' she says. 'I love it. It's so elegant.'

I have told her she can take anything she wants from my closet. And as Olivia and I have shared our clothes and makeup – as I have used her glittery eye shadow and she has borrowed my black tights – it has almost seemed as if we are converging. Once, I even tried on her bright red dress, and when I did, I felt like a different person.

'Will you put it on for me?' she asks, holding up the dress. 'It'll be romantic.'

'No, it won't. It's Ilan's mother's. She died of cancer. It would be disrespectful to her, and to Ilan, too.' There is silence for a moment. 'I can't believe you would suggest it,' I add.

'Maya, I didn't mean to be disrespectful, but Mrs Resnick is dead, and so is Ilan. It won't matter to either of them one way or the other. Please try on the dress. It's important to me.'

'It's important to me not to,' I protest.

But even as I complain, despite the sick feeling that washes over me, I begin unwrapping the wedding dress from its plastic sleeve.

Soon I am holding it up, so that it opens to me like a white tulip; stepping into it and adjusting my breasts in its bra cups; offering my bare back to Olivia so she can zip it up.

Again the silk stretches smooth across my stomach, just as it did after the operation. Once I am wearing the dress, Olivia asks me to lie down on the bed, and I do. She pushes my skirt up and to the side – the cloud of fabric in which Ilan's mother walked, his father once told me, as if she glided; in which she floated, years ago, to her groom.

With the skirt's layers cleared away, Olivia begins to tongue me.

I begin to squirm on the slippery silk of the dress's lining. It is only a matter of time. It is the usual surrender, I know: my special, patented surrender to the worst in me, taught to me by Ilan Resnick, who knew it well. What I am doing makes me want to cry, and yet I do not stop.

Soon I squirm not just on the silk lining but on my own wetness as well. Olivia's tongue on my clitoris is insistent as she pushes for the response she knows she will get, whether I like it or not. She flicks her tongue and I flinch noiselessly: I will not give her the satisfaction of moaning.

She pushes my thighs apart, pressing on them hard to spread them wide – just as I have done to her. She slips her tongue deeper and licks me faster and faster. All at once I tense, and then the spasm of feeling subsides. But still I am quiet. The struggle is won and lost silently as she feels the contractions of my orgasm fade away, hears my breathing return to normal.

Olivia rises, but a moment later, she stoops to kiss me. As she leans over me, like a bridegroom leaning, the small hand on Ilan's chain lowers, until it rests in the hollow above my sternum, with chain links pooling around it. As she kisses me, all I can feel is that small, cold hand.

Afterward she looks at me beatifically – thinking, perhaps, that the tears in my eyes are from pleasure, or at least from enlightenment. Thinking, perhaps, that this was just what I needed.

Before we go to sleep, she whispers to me, 'I love you. I've loved you for a long time now.' But I say nothing. I am so angry, I still cannot speak.

I sleep poorly and awaken shattered, sweating. Next to our bed, I see my wedding dress cast off on the floor – a stiff corset perched above a spreading, shining skirt, like the frozen curtsy of an invisible bride – and the cold, silent fury I felt last night comes back to me.

I rise and dress. All the clothes I pull on are soft: a loose black sweater with a high neck that covers my scars, gray fleece pants, slippers. I want to be a soft, quiet, small person at whom no one could feel anger, even as I do what I know I must.

I look around our bedroom and see all the small ways in which Olivia has changed it – the traces of

Ilan she has removed, the small things of hers she has introduced. I touch the shining fabrics, examine the graceful vases. I look at the large wooden jewelry box that we now share.

On the dresser, there are the photographs of me she has taken and framed. It is the series of us together that she took with a timer, to mimic the Prada store's mirror. In them, we were caught every few seconds – in the midst of laughter, in the midst of a kiss, in the midst of the past itself.

But I feel as I do when looking at photographs of the dead: the time these photos depict is so far away from me now. It is as if it recedes into the past before my eyes. The camera, on its timer, continues to click, but the subjects are gone; the dressing room, empty, is still recorded; the mirror still stutters its identical images.

I see how Olivia has carefully readied this place for us, as if it were a dollhouse built to hold a miniature life. And for me, I realize, she has carefully readied a life as well, the life I once wanted – as if it, too, were a room I have only to move into.

It all moves me – the photos, the objects, the care and the love. It is a beautiful life, the one Olivia has been building for me. But I am afraid I would be a stranger in it. My real life is still here with Ilan. Mr Resnick was right, after all, wasn't he? There is only one life. I already live it.

*　　*　　*

I leave the bedroom to find Olivia sitting at the breakfast table, paging through a book of photographs. As I approach her, I see they are of me. She strains her neck upward to kiss me, and I crane my neck downward and, for the last time, I let her.

'I can't do this,' I tell her bluntly, meaning to soften it but finally just saying it. 'I need to be by myself for a while. I need you to move out. I'm not ready.'

'Maya, this will pass. It's only jitters, like when you're getting married.'

'I didn't have jitters when I got married. I knew it was right. And this feels wrong to me.' A tear trickles down my cheek, and Olivia's face softens.

'Okay, maybe we went too fast,' she says. 'The wedding dress thing was a mistake, and I'm sorry. We can take it more slowly, and just date for a while. I'll move out. I love you, Maya. I don't want you to do anything you're not ready for. Maybe it was too soon.'

'You're not understanding me. I don't think we can date, not now. I think I need to be alone for a while, maybe permanently.'

'I want you to know, I know what this is about. It's about Ilan.' She is so furious she is shaking.

'It's not about him, it's about me for a change.'

'No, you're lying – I can tell it's him. We could have gotten a new apartment together, but you stay

207

here because of him. You certainly have the money to get another place, I see those statements.'

'Nothing here is private, is it? Not my wedding dress, or my writing, or my money.'

'Stop it! You're just trying to sidetrack me. Listen to me. You could have a new life, but you choose to stay here, because *he* lived here. You keep your job because *he* used to work there, when you could easily get a better one. I don't understand it. I treat you so much better than he ever did.'

'I know you do.'

'So what is it I have to do to get you to love me?' She has been raising her voice, but now she drops it. 'I wish you would tell me,' she whispers.

'I'm sorry, I really am. I know you must feel like I wasn't truthful all these months, but I've been trying to fight it. I didn't really know until now. I still feel married. I can't be with anyone else until I don't feel that way anymore.'

She collects herself, stands, and draws herself up in anger. 'Fine, stay with him, you deserve each other.' I notice that she, too, has taken to speaking of him almost as if he were alive.

As she leaves, I watch her hesitate as she considers slamming the door. Then I hear the click as she changes her mind and pulls it, with precision, shut.

*   *   *

In the evening, I am surprised when she returns.

'I want to sleep next to you,' she says. 'I have nowhere else to go.'

She starts crying again, in great gasps of sobs.

'There's your studio, isn't there?' I know how cold I sound, but I wish powerfully now that she would leave. With the wedding dress, she went too far; I can't forget about it, or get over it.

'There's not even a mattress at the studio,' she reminds me. 'I sold everything, remember?'

'Okay, you can stay tonight. But it has to be the last time. Tomorrow I'll help you find another place, and we'll get you some furniture.'

In bed, she reaches for me, but I push her away. With choked sobs, she cries again, with her back turned to me.

I don't comfort her. I don't want to give her false hope, and I am distracted by my own wish to be alone.

We each sleep near an edge of the bed that night, each wrapped in a separate white sheet – allowing enough room between us for a third person, even one as large as a man, to lie.

When I awaken the next morning, she is gone. Her things are gone too – packed up and taken away. I feel both relief and sadness, and beneath them, a strange, irrational dread – the same dread I felt with Ilan near the end. I try to ignore it; without fully knowing the reason for it, I do not know what I can do to quiet it.

That afternoon, I open the window and hear a little girl crying outside, in the playground across the street. I listen for a long time. It is eerily as if the sobs to which I listen are somehow my own, remembered from some lost and long ago childhood day, or intuited from some unhappy future – perhaps a near future, brought to me by a strange mirror that is the reverse of the Prada store's, a mirror of what is to come.

Yet it is only coincidence; this girl does not cry to me or for me, does she? It's simply that she happens, outside my window, to cry.

Still I listen, as if in memory or to a prophecy. I listen to bring the pain of hearing the little girl to the point just before I myself would have to cry out from it – it is another knife, another pressing down, another moment of wondering if a deep enough cut could open me. Finally, just before the tears would have begun, I close the window.

That night, in the silent apartment, I take my journals out from where I locked them away, in Ilan's desk. It is the first time in weeks that I have felt safe enough to do so.

I open the most current of the journals and begin to write. As always, I write about Ilan – and to him, as well. My journal entry for the night is this one:

This is a love letter, make no mistake. Ilan, my love for you is not deserved, it simply is. I carry it with me like a stone.

I've learned what you already knew, what you had known ever since you were a child: if you love someone and they die, and you cannot speak to them beforehand, you end up speaking to them afterward forever. I know now what you meant when you said you learned more about your mother every year, even though she'd died long ago. Each day I learn more about you.

Since you died, I've written like someone possessed, and now I am close to finishing. I am so glad of that – for I long to stop writing and sleep, so I can dream you on me, dream you in me once again.

I fall asleep knowing I will dream of Ilan, and I do. But a few hours later, while it is still pitch-black, I am awakened by the sound of a key turning in the loft's door.

Hearing the slight noise, I can barely think straight. A few seconds ago I was asleep, curled into myself compact as a seashell. My mind races with panic.

I hear a man's tread, similar to yours but lighter, as if you were now the ghost I have wished you to be. For a second I wonder if it is your father – he still has a key – but then I realize he could never walk so easily, so steadily.

It is then that I see her, moving soundlessly through the single sharp-edged shaft of light that a streetlight casts into the loft. Her head makes a small dark silhouette like the head of a boy. Her long hair, for the first time since I have known her, is pinned up.

I make out gradually, with increasing unease, what she is wearing: a man's dark suit, a white shirt, and men's loafers, their leather glossy. Clothes from your closet, Ilan – the small one I never open now. A black belt of yours too, fastened at the last notch but still loose on her. And in her hand, your small silver gun.

The box had been left unlocked, unprotected, I realize. I had locked the desk drawers that held my notebooks, but not the one that held the gun. She had only to open it while I was asleep, take it with her one day – yesterday? long ago? – and bring it here now.

As she stands there in your clothes, holding the gun uncertainly in front of her, the resemblance to you hurts and scares me. It is very dark, she is only a few inches shorter than you were, and the loose shirt that hides her breasts conspires, along with her narrow hips, to make her body almost resemble yours.

'If you want him,' she announces, standing before me in the slant of the light, 'you can have him. I can be him.' Her eyes are puffy, red from crying, unfocused, but the set of her jaw is determined: she will not give up.

'No,' I tell her. 'Please don't. It's not going to solve anything.'

'Take off your sweater,' she instructs me. Obediently I pull it, soft and white, over my head. The air is cold on my skin. A few strands of white wool have stuck to my lower back, my sternum – places where, as soon as I saw her, I began to sweat with anxiety.

'Take off your pants. Now.'

I pull them down and step out of them. Despite myself, I am excited by her commands.

'Your panties.'

I slip them off.

'Your bra.'

And I am naked.

She takes three lengths of cord out of her pants pocket – the cords from your silk robe, she must have found them in the closet.

'Tie up your legs. Now. One to each bedpost.'

She unnerves me, but I have not changed: I do what I am told, sexually. And I even strangely enjoy it, in the midst of my fear. Ilan, I have not been so aroused since you were alive.

I tie one leg to each corner of the metal frame at the foot of the bed, obediently pulling the cords tight. Once I am safely tied up, Olivia puts the gun on the side table, and with your black cloth, she blindfolds me. Then she takes the last of the cords and ties my hands to each other, and then to the bed frame – in the same style you preferred. She must have read my journals, after all.

I hear her unzip the pants she is wearing. And then it is you, Ilan, not her, whom I envision. With the blindfold on, I can finally see you. Rather than becoming you, as Olivia intends, she only gives you back to me. Meant to be an exorcism, it is instead a summoning.

I feel my mind opening to you, like a sleeping eye. The material of your pants moves, soft, against my thighs as you push inside me. I want to reach for your crisp white shirt the way I used to, so it buckles, starched, in my hands – to unbutton it so I can touch the smooth skin of your chest, its scattering of hair. I test my hands against their restraints but I can't break free. I am so frustrated I want to cry.

I open my legs until the cords are tested. I want you inside me as deeply as is physically possible, and also more deeply than that. I enjoy your thrusting, Ilan. I moan with it. You alternate between cupping the entire breast firmly and pinching, with two fingers, each nipple – the way you used to. I squirm beneath you, the way I used to. It is all the same.

In minutes I climax, I feel you climax with me,

and then I feel you go still and withdraw. Now that you are back, I wonder what it is you want from me.

Olivia pulls my blindfold off abruptly. She seems very angry; I think she senses how far away my thoughts have been. She slips the pants down, and there is the plastic, complete with veins and ridges, with the slight suture on the side like the seam on a Barbie doll's foot; there is the harness, the harsh mesh of the straps. She rips the harness off, zips the pants closed.

It wasn't you, after all, of course it wasn't. And yet it was, I could swear it; I believe it.

The white shirt hangs loosely around her. She takes it off, and I see that beneath it she is still wearing your chain – its guiding, seductive, trailing hand.

She pulls on a fluorescent yellow T-shirt she has left here, and, one by one, she takes out the barrettes that hold her hair up – their layered green sequins orderly and strange as the scales on a mermaid's tail. Then she pulls her hair down violently into its usual wash of red.

She sits on the bed besides me daintily, cross-legged – furious but femininely so. She no longer imitates you. But she makes no move to untie me and from this I see it is not over: not yet.

'You read my journals,' I accuse her. 'You read them and then you followed them like a manual.'

'I looked at one page, just like I said I did. I kept my promises to you, Maya, all of them. I love you.'

'I love you too, but I can't be with you. I have to have another life. I don't like this, I don't want it anymore.'

'Really? For someone who didn't want it, you seemed to enjoy it a lot. You want Ilan back, but when I give him back to you, you balk. Fuck you. I did everything you wanted. And you're still going to leave me, aren't you?'

'I can't let my life just replay itself like this.'

'But it's supposed to. Ilan said it would.'

'What do you mean he said it would?'

'He told me you'd fall in love with me. He said it would be hard at first, but I should be persistent. At first I was skeptical, but he showed me the photos, told me stories. I started to want you. I started to think about you all the time. I read all your articles.'

'Did you know he was going to kill himself?' I ask, horrified.

'No, of course not, he said he was leaving you, that's all. I wanted to be the woman – I wanted to be next. I even dyed my hair so I fit the ad. I used to be blonde. I gained a little weight too. It took a lot of peanut butter and ice cream.' She giggles slightly.

I look at her red hair, garish against her yellow T-shirt, at the almost invisible line of blond at her part; I remember the bright red dress. And I think of the faint stretch marks on her breasts and thighs,

216

marks of a time when she was thinner. I should have seen it; I don't know how I did not.

'You're scaring me,' I tell her.

'You should be flattered. Ilan wanted someone else to love you, and he interviewed a lot of women, and he chose me.'

'When you showed up on my doorstep, it was all an act?'

'You were acting too, Maya. You wouldn't even tell me he was dead, at first.'

'You lied to me.'

'So did you. We lied to each other, and we wanted each other. And we got each other. Don't you see that that's good? We could live happily ever after, if you would only let us,' she pleads. 'If you want me to be Ilan for you, I can do that. I've shown you I can. I can do it again. Let me show you.'

'No,' I tell her quietly. 'I can't, I don't want it.'

'That's not the right answer,' she replies calmly. I look into her eyes and see the shine of some drug there – in her inability fully to focus, her faraway look. It is as if she is trying to think, to reason out a difficult problem, her forehead wrinkled, her expression concerned. With her huge, dilated pupils, she moves in her own world, unfeeling – as if she could hum or whistle to herself as she decides what to do with me.

*   *   *

I begin to plead with Olivia, but she tells me to be quiet, and she puts the blindfold back on. Something terrible will happen now, I can feel it.

I think of screaming, but I realize it would do me no good. The street outside is deserted at this hour, and the double-paned glass of the closed windows is meant to block out sound; that was why Ilan's father chose it. When the little girl's cries in the playground disturbed me, I could simply close the window to silence them. My cries, too, will not be heard.

I hear the bed creak slightly as she settles down beside me.

'Maya, do you like the razor blades best,' she asks me, 'or do you like this?'

She thrusts quick and cold and hard between my spread legs. I feel the gun inside me.

'Please. You're scaring me to death.'

'That's what you like, isn't it? A little fear? Why don't you come for me?'

She pushes the gun farther, thrusts inside me with it.

'You always used to come for him this way. Why not for me?'

'Untie me,' I plead. 'Please let me go.'

'Ilan wouldn't have. Why should I?'

For once I am not excited but very afraid, sweaty and shaking. I am beginning to feel as if I am within a new kind of dream now, not a dream of falling or flying but a dream of being frozen – the kind you are powerless to stop.

'Ilan said the only way to get through to you was pain. The more pain, the better. The woman who wouldn't cut you hard enough – he said you wanted her to go further. At first I didn't believe him, but he's right, isn't he? You *are* looking for pain. You love it. You go over his death in your mind every single day just to hurt yourself.'

'No, I was relieved when that woman stopped, I didn't want her to hurt me. Please, this is making me afraid, it's not turning me on. You know me, remember? You were right about me, and he was wrong. I love you, Olivia.' I try hard to mask my fear.

'No you don't,' she says under her breath, as if she were speaking only to herself. I have begun to lie now and she knows it.

She pushes the gun into me even harder than he did now, and faster.

'Please stop,' I tell her. Then I tense for another thrust, but I never feel it. Instead she hesitates. She withdraws the gun, and I hear metal against metal as it is replaced in its box.

'I wish I'd never met you,' she says. 'I wish it had never come to this.'

Eagerly I interrupt her. 'You love me, you don't want to hurt me, right? We can go back to what we used to have, in the beginning.'

She is tempted, thinks about it, but finally says no. 'I'm going to lose you whatever I do now, I can see that. So I might as well see how it felt to be him. To make you happy. To give you what you really want.'

That tone in her voice: I've never heard her be sarcastic before. She had been eager, sweet, ingenuous – even embarrassing. Until she met Ilan; until she met me.

I struggle against her but it is no contest, for I am already tied up, and soon she binds around my mouth the familiar gag. And for the first time it happens, as it never happened in all the games you played with me, Ilan: I can neither see nor speak.

She adjusts the blindfold over my eyes, to make sure I cannot see even a sliver of light. And that is how I know it is ending.

It is not a razor blade this time, but a long knife – the one from our kitchen, I imagine, slipped from its wooden sheath. Against my wrists, I feel the range of its stroke, the sharpness of the blade. I feel Olivia gently trace the cuts on my arms, feel them begin to reopen.

She moves my head into her lap, to draw the blade across my neck, first tentatively but then with a stronger pull – like a cellist delicately, firmly drawing sound forth from the strings of a still body with her bow.

With one more cut, my throat will open easily to the air. In a moment I will hear it gasp like a second mouth, hear the momentary suck and gurgle of air and then hear the silence as, with blood, the airstream is overcome. I will be drowning, after all.

I know I must do it in a few seconds, with the advantage of surprise. At my wrists I stretch the cords, and it is agony but I wrench them to stretch the silk as far as it can go, pressing my fingers together to make my hands as long and slender as I can, and then twisting them out.

I slip one hand out, and then the other. Still blind, I grab for Olivia, and in my hand I feel her hair, which I have so often touched in bed. I grab its strands, pull her head down, and she cries out. The knife clatters to the floor.

I rip the blindfold off and then the gag. I see the gout of her red hair still in my hand. Still tipped with blond, it has been torn out at the root. I open my hand in horror and let it fall.

I strain to reach the knife on the floor and in a second I have it. With it, I slice cleanly through the ties that still bind my legs. I am free; we are even, now.

She is still frozen, slowed by some drug, stilled by surprise for the few seconds I need to try to escape her. I run for my life, an animal's flight.

The door opens smoothly and I slam it behind me. In a second I am in the elevator. I watch, as if in a movie, the doors close until they show only a slice of Olivia's dazed, furious face, then nothing.

The elevator, with agonizing slowness, travels downward. I notice then that the cuts on my wrists, the older cuts, have stopped bleeding. But the cuts on my throat still bleed a bit. I am lucky, though: the cuts never got to that crucial depth, the bleeding never increases. A tiny veil of skin keeps the blood in me at bay – like the ribbon that held together the severed neck of the girl in the fairy tale. Yet the veil holds.

There is no other way down, I realize – no fire escape, but only a rope ladder stashed away in a closet, and Olivia won't know about it. I jam an umbrella between the elevator doors, and slip into the basement to find old clothes to put on, too afraid to slip out into the city's darkness while I am naked and bleeding, even as desperate to leave here as I am.

Ilan's clothes are in the nearest boxes – his father stored some of them there after he died – and so it is in his T-shirt and trousers that I venture back to the ground floor. There I see that the elevator doors, closing and closing again, have crushed the umbrella and somehow ejected it; it lies broken on the floor. I hear the elevator rising.

*   *   *

I run out into the darkened streets of downtown. Tribeca always seems deserted to me – its wide streets too broad for its few residents – and never more deserted than now.

Running for my life, I move smoothly and silently – in the way I used to row in college, when the sound of my oars was like a flutter, when it was almost like no sound at all: the sound of closing a venetian blind, or of a bird's wing, tucked in a second ago, expanding to prepare for flight.

I do not make it five blocks before I hear her behind me. I look quickly to see if she is holding the gun, and she is.

She is still a block and a half away from me, but she raises it at me, and takes aim. I dive to the pavement, scraping my arms and knees, and roll to the side, behind a Dumpster.

I hear the shot ping off something and reverberate. Then I hear someone in a high window nearby, looking down on us, scream.

Inside a nearby doorway, I see a hinged grate. I open it and slip inside. It is a small stone room, some restaurant's odd storage space. I sit next to wine bottles and stacked boxes, and I hold my breath. I can only hope she will not find me.

Olivia slows when she gets near the Dumpster, as if she is looking for me. I see her shoes – Ilan's shoes – and through my shock, the insanity of it all comes home to me again. Who will be my true assassin, of the two?

She pries at the grate and I hold my breath. But she decides against it, returns to the street and picks up her pace. She must believe I have somehow – under cover of this row of skewed gargantuan Dumpsters which blocked the sidewalk and obscured her view – moved on. I hear her continue running, and eventually, with relief, I hear her swift footsteps fade.

I wait awhile, to ensure she won't double back. As I wait in the small crawlspace, I press a hand into my own blood, and I place its print on the dirty stone wall next to me. Then I draw the print downward, all the while thinking of Ilan's smeared print on the wall of our apartment – still there, invisible.

A few minutes later, I feel brave enough to venture out. Near the Dumpster, I find the gun; she must have tossed it aside. I check it and realize why: it is empty now.

I head back to our apartment – believing it is the one place she won't expect to find me. I am cautious, entering, but I know she has no weapon now, and I cannot imagine that she would have given up looking in the direction she believed I'd run.

Once inside the apartment, I make sure she is not there, and I use the special dead bolt, which cannot be opened from outside.

I think of calling the police, but I know that if I turn Olivia in, she is likely to tell the press everything that's happened. She'll try to shame me, and I may lose my career, my reputation – even the trusts, which I remember that Mr Resnick can still revoke. This might, I think, be just enough to convince him to do so.

And so I do not call. Instead I wash my cuts – wash the blood from them and see how deep they really go, swab them and bandage them and camouflage them with a scarf.

Then I call a locksmith, who arrives at six a.m. to change all the locks. He gives me the new keys, and the walls of the loft at once become a physical barrier that will protect me. I pay him, and am glad to pay him. I survived; I have returned.

Though I am glad to have the new locks, I do not really believe Olivia will return here. Instead I believe that after failing to find me, she'll collapse, exhausted, to sleep in her studio. Then the next morning, I imagine, she will awaken with shame and horror at where her life has gone, what it has become.

As the drug evaporates out of her blood, she will blink and be appalled. As if from a dream, she will awaken – as I did, in the end, with Ilan – in disbelief at what has occurred, questioning if it could have been real, if it actually happened.

*　　*　　*

When the locksmith leaves, I go up to our roof to see the sun rise as if it were a symbol, or a song.

From there, I watch the city perform its early-morning orderings, its careful arrangings – as its trucks are unloaded, its newspapers slipped into their places on newsstands for their headlines to quietly blare, its flowers arrayed outside its grocery stores in their plastic barrels. For the first time in a long time, I am glad to be alive, more glad than I can say. I whirl around to survey every perspective, to see the life on every nearby street.

And there is Olivia. She faces me, from the far corner of the roof, like a terrible reflection of myself. She is closer to the door that leads down to the loft than I am, and so she has me trapped up here. In her hand, there is the long knife.

She must have doubled back after all, beaten me back to the apartment and then waited for me here on the roof – waited patiently until I arrived here. Did she know me well enough to know that I would want to come up here to see the city, to remind myself that other, happier lives continue around me?

Olivia walks toward the door that leads to the down staircase, and stands in front of it, blocking it. There is no other way down.

'Let it go,' I tell her. 'It's over now.'

'It's been over for you for a long time,' she says.

'For me, it never will be over. I know you locked me out – I heard you talking to that man – but it's not that easy to keep me out. You're never going to be able to keep me out.'

We stand there like that, each against her own small backdrop of buildings, each exhausted and determined, each still dressed in Ilan's clothes – as if the part of him that loved life were confronting the part that loved death. It occurs to me that the last time this happened, it was death that won.

It is then that I remember the heavy, empty gun in my pocket.

'You don't love me anymore,' she declares mournfully.

'It's not a crime. I don't have to love you.'

'But I have to love you. He made me.'

'You can stop. He's not as powerful as you think.'

I back away from her, to the furthest corner of the roof, and there I carefully slip the gun out of my pocket, lift it, and point it toward her.

'It's empty,' she tells me.

'Not anymore. I knew you might come back. Why do you think I have it up here?'

I begin to walk, with a measured pace, toward her. The bluff of my life – but I know how to suppress emotion, I remind myself. If I had not learned how, I would have broken down. I would have stayed in the psychiatric ward forever. I am far away, I tell myself; I am untouchable. I cannot die, because

I am not here. I am inside my still, calm mind instead.

'If you leave, I won't call the police,' I explain to Olivia. 'I'll let everything drop. But if you don't leave, if you try again, I'm going to have to shoot you, not fatally, but I will. And after that, I'll go to the police. I won't have a choice – I'm going to have to explain why I did it. And then it will all be over – no more shows, no more clients. I'm not the only one with a life to lose, Olivia.'

'You were my life.'

'You have a life without me.' Now or never: I point the gun at her. It convinces her, at least, to back away. Then, when I judge she is far enough away from me, I lean against the door, still facing her, to push it open.

It does not give – she must have locked it while I watched the city, to trap me up here with her. She still has the key, I realize: it's the only lock the locksmith didn't change. It made sense: after all, no one could get to the roof before getting past the new locks first. Except, of course, if someone was already there.

Watching her carefully, I slip the key out of my pocket. There is no other way: I'll have to turn my back on her for a moment. I can't open the door and turn the key at the same time.

'Go to the far corner,' I command her.

'Scared of me?' she taunts.

'I'm scared, but I'm going to do it anyway. Move or I'll shoot you. I mean it.'

She moves, and she is as far away as she can be, and I twist the key as fast as I can, and she runs at me with the knife.

In seconds, though, the door is open, and I am through it, and as I try to push it closed, I hear her body fall heavily against it, the knife clatter down.

I fight her – her lacquered fingernails trying to get purchase on the doorjamb, her shoulder firm against the door – for the last few inches of space, the inches between closed and open, between life and death.

With all the strength that is left in me, I push. But she is stronger, and has the advantage of pushing inward, when I must resist the naturally opening door, with its oiled hinge and its smooth swing.

I feel myself shifting backward, pushed back as the door is pushed back toward me. Her full hands appear, grabbing at the door's edge. In a moment, she will be through.

But then I feel a jolt of emotion, of true fear: I imagine I am closing Ilan's coffin, and it is that strange fantasy – the bony hand, the struggling skeleton – that turns revulsion into strength. I throw myself against the door, and I hear the satisfying click by which it shuts and then I hold it there.

Suddenly, strangely, in the midst of this chaos, I remember the advertisement: 5'9", 130. We are

229

equally matched adversaries, Olivia and I. But one of us very much wants to live, and the other does not want quite as passionately to kill her, and the story of my life, in the end, is that: the story of that last push, of the life in me.

With the force of that last push, I close and lock the door. I know she can unlock it – she still has the key – but not before I can flee downstairs, lock myself behind the new lock, safe from her in the apartment. And so I do.

I am surprised to find that I have plenty of time. With the door locked against her, Olivia seems to give up; I do not even hear the key slipping into the lock, I never hear it begin to turn, as I skitter downstairs, almost falling in my haste to reach safety.

For hours, Olivia does not leave – I listen carefully at the loft's door, but I never hear her tread on the stairs. Then, finally, from my window, I see her walk out onto the street.

Looking down at her lovely hair in disarray, I remember the first time I ever saw her – as she scrutinized the tiny piece of paper in her hand, nervous, making sure she had our address right. I remember her pink sweater, her red hair: the fraud, the passion. I wonder if, in this moment, she is remembering too, remembering our beginning.

I wonder if, even leaving, she still feels the spell; I

wonder if she is still inside it. I wonder how I ever managed to get free.

That first night in Rome, I do not – though I am tempted to do so – return to the hotel Ilan and I once visited, where he pressed me to the wall. I find another hotel, and in its sink, with a bottle, I become a blonde there, as if I were one of the women he glanced at on our honeymoon, but never touched.

Some change must inaugurate my new life, and I decide that it will be this – this superficial one, as if by appearing different I can hope to be different. A trick, but one that might work, for something has to.

I am a pretty blonde, I decide, but more than that, as a blonde I am different. I seem happier, as if the lighter hair lightens me. My white smile flashes out, my blond hair shines, I am suddenly very American – a girl with a charmed life, who felt entitled, who never cried, who was always loved, who was never lonely. One of my half sisters, perhaps; certainly not myself.

I cannot love Ilan my whole life, I know it now – it would be too lonely, or too lethal, or both. If I learned anything from Olivia, it was that. But I cannot quite leave him behind either. And so I decide I will walk along the streets of this foreign city as he once did – looking at its women as he would have. He was correct: they are beautiful.

Though the men are beautiful too, and I desire them, I feel I need to be with women before I can be with a man again. Before I leave Ilan, I must first become him.

And so I do become him, and I find it pleasurable, pleasurable in the extreme. I avail myself of the women, and I enjoy it, as he would have, and they open to me, as they would have to him.

One night I am with two beautiful women in the white expanse of my hotel bed, and as we writhe I realize, with a shock of loneliness, that he is no longer with me, even as a ghost. There is no one watching.

As I realize this, my pleasure comes to me. I contract and release, kiss and end my kiss, shudder and fall still. I believe it may finally be over.

Afterward, the two women – both Italian, and speaking little English – do not leave: they both sleep next to me, and in the morning I feel spoiled, for it all happens once again.

It should not be permitted to happen again – Ilan, directing it, would never have allowed that – but it does. It is a dream but now I am the one dreaming it. It is a dream of flying, and not a dream of falling. It is a dream in which I am happy, as I have rarely been in life.

On the dream platform I meet these two women

and all we do is try to give each other pleasure; there is no undercurrent of sadness, no tainted bargain, no inevitable end. In my heart, as I spend hours with them, something breaks, and I know it is a constraint breaking. It is the feeling of finally moving past that claustrophobic love that has kept my mind in my half of that double grave, long before my body is due to settle there.

Still, one final doubt remains in me: I wonder, as I watch the women – as I tongue their nipples, lick them so suddenly they startle and moan, as I use my hard-won expertise for their pleasure – I wonder whether I want them or whether, in wanting them, I am merely remembering him.

It is hardly a new confusion; I have never, I realize, been entirely able to tell my desire from his – not since the first day I saw him, when he asked me, 'Are you waiting for me?'

I was not, I think now – answering his question finally, so many years after it was asked. I was not waiting for him. I was waiting for myself – for my soul, in some sense – but it had yet to arrive, and so I took on his instead.

When the women leave – the women I know are the very ones that Ilan, too, would have selected, assessed, considered, seduced – I begin to speak to Ilan in my mind, as if to settle things between us once and for all.

I have thought about it all, Ilan – everything that happened – for a long time, on the plane and afterward, and now I believe it is all clear to me. Only now do I see that my story has two authors, and one of them is you.

It was a test for me, wasn't it? A test of faith, of sorts.

Once again you must have enjoyed the process of choosing among the women, wished it would never end. You chose Olivia for a special quality, I know it now: a certain instability, a dark capacity. I never questioned her past, the depth of her need, the drugs, her dependence on me. I never questioned anything about her, not really, because you had sent her – when that was the very reason I should have looked closer.

It's funny, but I still believe that the happiness she offered me – the happiness you offered me, through her – was real. It was not a false promise. It was real as long as I could accept it. But if I could not, if I remained in love with you despite all her efforts, you knew she wouldn't be able to adjust to that. You knew she might even be jealous enough to prefer killing me to losing me.

And if I still loved you, then wasn't death what I wanted – what I deserved? How else could we be reunited, you and I? Once Romeo dies, Juliet must soon take up the knife. It is for her to finish it. If she loves him, she will choose to die with him; she will not want to live.

That's why you told Olivia, though she'd hoped it was a lie, that pain, and even death, were what I really sought. I was your Juliet, and I loved you more than life, so you thought darkness would be what I truly longed for.

You even told Olivia the details, exactly how to do it – and she was weak, as you chose her to be, and she followed you, just as I once did. You opened the way, Ilan, you foresaw and foreordained it all. The pain you coaxed from me while you were alive survived you. After your death, it only grew, until it was almost the death of me.

In some sense, every suicide is also a murder, and yours was more of a murder than I could ever have guessed. It's funny, all those months, I still imagined myself alive. The only thing you did not predict was that in the end, I might escape – I might not turn out to be the victim you believed me to be.

I had been such a perfect victim, Ilan; it was an understandable mistake. But while I had no gift for happiness, no gift for the exercise of will, I finally had a gift for life. And perhaps that is the most important gift of all.

How sad, how bitter, it is to understand one's life only afterward, when it is too late to go back and change it. And yet, in another way, I know it is not too late for me – for I've survived your death, and my youth, and our love. I lived your death without quite suffering it.

The cut did not go quite deep enough for me, though it came so close. There was a veil of skin, a ribbon – a faith or hope – that intervened at the last minute. There was a grate, an opening, a gun that held one bullet too few. And more than this, there was a girl, eighteen years old, who learned to row, who became strong long before you met her, and later, when she had to, could run.

I am still that girl. And so I have this life, the life I'm left with. What I will do with it remains to be seen.

The next day, it is time for my interview. Looking at the newspaper, I realize that it is my twenty-fifth birthday, and that I had totally forgotten it was coming. I whistle 'Happy Birthday' to myself and wonder if the same tune is used to celebrate in Italy, or a different one. I take off my wedding ring and put it in my pocket.

I finally use the cell phone number the actor gave me so long ago; I make the call and he picks up immediately.

When I meet him, he is in the hotel room, alone again. This time, he has no secrets, I can see it in his face. It is me he wants to see; he has nothing to reveal but that alone. This will not be an interview, not exactly.

He sits in a rickety chair and motions for me to come close to him, and I do. Once I have approached, I can sense that he is waiting, and I know he is not waiting for me to speak, but to move: to move toward him.

I swing one leg across his broad waist and mount him, and in this way I conduct the interview – asking the questions I have prepared. As he answers, he does not touch me, except to keep our crotches pressed together. I press against him hard, breathing hard.

We make a sliding, limited, grainy connection through our clothes. It is so modest, so furtive, this grinding, that it takes me back to a time before Ilan, the year I was eighteen. I begin then to remember the two boys I was with before Ilan, and to believe there could be someone after.

The actor is more than willing to go further. He raises my shirt up, unhooks my bra. As he licks my breasts, gentle with my nipples, his touch is nothing like Ilan's, and I, responding to him, am nothing like the way I used to be.

It is with his own belt that I tie him up – his hands bound together behind the chair – and he does not protest it, and that is the way I ride him.

As I move on him, I wonder if I will someday see him, and not only hear him, cry. And I think of how

Ilan never cried – never except on the single day when he finally told me about his mother; and how even on that day, I never saw his tears, I could never be sure.

It occurs to me then that strength and power can be a mistake, and that there can be a kind of strength and power, too, in the ability simply to open, to be courageous enough to be known. It was a strength Ilan lacked, and one I would like to begin learning.

As I move up and down on the actor, I know there is no guarantee I will ever see him again. But in my heart, I believe I will.

I lean down to kiss him, with the feeling that we are beginning. There is another life.

THE END

THE SEXUAL LIFE OF CATHERINE M.
by Catherine Millet

'One of the most explicit books about sex ever written by a woman'
Edmund White

The Sexual Life of Catherine M. is the autobiography of a well-known Parisian art critic who likes to spend nights in the singles clubs of Paris and in the Bois de Boulogne where she has sex with a succession of anonymous men. Unlike many contemporary women writers, there is no guilt in Millet's narrative, no chronicles of use and abuse: on the contrary, she has no regrets about a life of sexual activity. Catherine Millet's writing is a subtle reflection on the boundaries of art and life and she uses her insights on the role of the body in modern art to set the scene for her multiple sexual encounters.

A penomenal bestseller in France and in all other countries in which it has been published, *The Sexual Life of Catherine M.* is very much a manifesto of our times – when the sexual equality of women is a reality and where love and sex have gone their own separate ways. Like the *Story of O*, it is a truly shocking book that captures a decisive moment in our sexual history.

'I thought it was the most honest book I had ever read on the subject of sex'
Rowan Pelling, *Daily Telegraph*

'A brilliant testimony of life spent at the sexual front line'
Independent on Sunday

'Unabashed erotica . . . a straight-talking romp catalogued with savage wit by a Parisian intellectual'
The Scotsman

'Millet writes extremely well . . . it is neither pornography nor her coy younger sister, erotica, but a work of libertine philosophy'
Times Literary Supplement

0 552 77172 4

STORY OF O
by Pauline Réage

One of the most famous erotic novels of all time.

'A rare thing, a pornographic book well written and
without a trace of obscenity'
Graham Greene

'A highly literary and imaginative work, the brilliance of
whose style leaves no-one in doubt whatever of the
author's genius . . . a profoundly disturbing book, as well
as a black tour-de-force'
Spectator

'Here all kinds of terrors await us, but like a baby taking
its mother's milk all pains are assuaged. Touched by the
magic of love, everything is transformed. *Story of O* is a
deeply moral homily'
J. G. Ballard

'Cool, cruel, formalistic fantasy about a woman subjected
– at the price of the great love of her life – to the gamut of
male sado-masochistic urges'
Birmingham Post

0 552 08930 3